This dangerously handsome, effortlessly stylish half-demon is Chicago's foremost paranormal investigator. With magical aptitude and specialized weapons, Luther Cross will handle your supernatural problems… for the right price.

THE MYTH HUNTER

All the legends of the world have some element of truth to them. And to track down those legends, there are the myth hunters. Some, like Elisa Hill, are explorers, trying to learn more about the world. And some are soldiers of fortune, whose only goal is profit and exploitation, no matter the risk.

INFERNUM

A shadowy, globe-spanning network of operatives run by the mysterious power broker known as Dante. They hold allegiance to no one, existing as rogues on the fringes of society. No matter the job, Infernum has an operative to execute it—provided you have the means to pay for it!

VANGUARD

The world has changed. A mysterious event altered the genetic structure of humanity, granting a small percentage of the population superhuman powers. A small team of these specials has been formed to deal with potential threats. Paragon—telekinetic powerhouse; Zenith—hyper-intelligent automaton; Shift—shape-changing teenager; Wraith—teleporting shadow warrior; Sharkskin—human/shark hybrid. Led by the armored Gunsmith, they are Vanguard!

Visit PercivalConstantine.com for an up-to-date list of titles!

Published by Pulp Corner Press

http://www.percivalconstantine.com

A MORNINGSTAR NOVEL

LUCIFER BOUND

BY PERCIVAL CONSTANTINE

CHAPTER 1

I t has often been said that the full moon brings out the crazies. And this particular summer night in Chicago proved no different. Even at three in the morning, the night air was warm. The gatehouse for Rosehill Cemetery had the appearance of a gothic cathedral. But in the middle of the night, the gate was supposed to be closed.

A man dressed in a white suit appeared seemingly out of nowhere, his yellow eyes like embers illuminating the darkness. He approached the gate and examined where it had been broken into. A crude job, which suggested he wasn't dealing with experienced professionals here.

He glanced up at the moon and sighed. Three AM—the Witching Hour. Or in some circles, the Devil's Hour (a term he wasn't very fond of himself). The time of day when the veil between worlds was at its thinnest. And when summoning rituals were at their most effective.

With his hands in his pockets, he calmly walked past the broken gate, as if he were just on a leisurely, Sunday morning stroll through a park. One would have almost expected him to whistle a tune.

A few steps in and he stopped, noticing something on the edge of the grass. The man in white knelt down and reached out, running his fingers over the tire tread. It was fresh. Made just before he arrived. While his fingers brushed over the track, images flashed in his mind.

The trunk opening. A child, bound at the wrists and ankles with tape over his mouth. The boy resists, but there are two men holding him. His thrashing means nothing to them. A third person waits at the trunk, holding it open. The boy is thrown inside. The trunk slams shut.

He stood upright and closed his eyes. Though to the rest of the world he was still as a statue, what he actually did was reach out with his power. He had a kind of sixth sense that allowed him to expand his perceptions and feel for supernatural energies.

And he could get a sense of something in this cemetery. It was very weak, which again reinforced his theory that these were amateurs. But the forces they were messing with were by no means benign. If he didn't stop these idiots before they completed their ritual, there was no telling what sort of chaos they might unleash.

He wasn't about to let that happen. The Astaroth affair had caused him enough problems. Things were now on a tenuous footing between him and the angels, and he had no desire to draw any more attention to himself.

The car was a red sedan and had seen better days. A bumper sticker on the back read "WHAT WOULD SATAN DO?" He almost wanted to chuckle—they were about to find out.

It was parked haphazardly in front of the Rosehill Mausoleum. At two stories—one partially underground— it was the largest mausoleum in the city. When he came to the steps leading up to the quartet of white columns, he got a clearer sense of the energies lurking inside.

The door had been pried open and he walked past it and into the main hall. His feet were soft as he moved across the marble floor, not making a single sound. The columns gave way to family tombs, the names etched across the walls in a grid-like formation.

His senses guided him through the mausoleum, towards the back east end of the building. Now he could hear voices echoing as he came closer. Three voices, in fact. Two male, but one was female, and clearly in command of the others. No screaming or crying, which could mean the boy was dead or just still gagged.

Their voices came from behind the doors leading to the John G. Shedd Chapel. He clapped his hands and rubbed them together. Then, with a gesture, the doors blew open and he strolled right through them.

A skylight was above them, bearing an intricate design of vines, and the moonlight filtered through the glass. The marble room had a series of benches arranged in a semi-square, with a podium standing before the Shedd family tomb. The design on the wall and in the chairs featured aquatic elements.

And in the center of that ring of benches, held down to the ground by the two young men, was the child. A boy of about eight years old. The young woman was standing at the podium, an intricately designed dagger in one hand, the other hand resting on an old grimoire.

"Who the hell are you?" asked one of the young men.

His head was nearly shaved, with just a thin stubble of hair across his scalp. The other had shaggy brown hair, and seemed like any average university student one could spot around the city. The girl was around eighteen or nineteen, with chin-length dark hair and blue eyes that looked upon him with fear and uncertainty.

"That's an interesting dagger you have there," said the man in white. "Judging by its design, the book you're reading, and the innocent child being held down on the floor, would I be wrong in assuming that you're trying to offer a sacrifice to summon a demon?"

"None of your business!" said the girl.

"On the contrary, I think it's very much my business… Caitlin."

What little color remained in her fair skin drained completely. She stammered for a reply, but nothing came out other than a series of noises.

"How do I know your name? Or how do I know that the bald one is Dave and the handsome brunette is Brock?"

The two men exchanged quick confused glances, and then looked at Caitlin. She didn't acknowledge them, just kept staring at the man in white.

"The answer to all these questions is quite simple. You wanted to summon a demon, well I am the first demon." He gave a bow as his yellow eyes simmered. "My name is Lucifer."

The dagger fell from Caitlin's hand and clattered on the ground. Dave and Brock both loosened their grips on the boy and slowly turned to fully face him. Caitlin staggered forward, coming closer to the Morningstar.

"It…it can't be…" she whispered. "My dark lord…? Is this really…have we been blessed by your presence?"

Her obsequious nature did little to calm the rage Lucifer felt building within him. In fact, it only increased his hatred for this woman and her two little lapdogs. He was now close enough to touch her, and so he reached out and brushed his hand over her cheek. She shivered in response and closed her eyes, an expression akin to arousal falling over her features.

Lucifer could see her memories flashing before him. A middle-class suburban girl, wanting to rebel against her religious parents. Turned to the black arts, but never accomplished anything other than the most elementary of spells. Floating a pencil for half a second, creating a spark to light a candle, but nothing beyond that. She simply lacked both the natural aptitude towards magic and the discipline to overcompensate for that deficit.

One of the interesting aspects of Lucifer's psychometric abilities was that they were not a one-way street. He was more than just a receiver of memories—he could also project his own memories or those he'd viewed into the mind of another. And they would feel those memories as if they had experienced them firsthand. Before he came to Rosehill, Lucifer had visited the boy's home and absorbed memories from his bed.

Lucifer grabbed a fistful of Caitlin's hair and pulled. She screamed and he placed his other hand on the side of her head, showing her just what the boy had felt as his favorite babysitter pulled him from the bed and kept yelling at him to shut up while her two boyfriends bound and gagged him. Caitlin could feel the boy's fear, and she shouted in feeble protest, just as he had.

"What did you do to her?" asked Brock, coming at him.

"I showed her what it feels like," said Lucifer. "Would you like to experience it as well?"

Brock attempted to charge the Morningstar, rushing at him and swinging his fists wildly. Lucifer moved lithely stepping out of the path of the punch, then pushed on

Brock's shoulder and let his own momentum send him stumbling forward and right into the wall.

Dave had picked up the knife and now pointed it at Lucifer. "D-don't make me do this! I'll fuck you up, man!"

Lucifer let out a sigh of exasperation. "Little man, do you have any concept of what the word 'immortal' means?"

"Nah, you're not him, you can't be!" shouted Dave.

"And what makes you say that?" asked Lucifer.

"Satan…he'd be cheering us on! He *wants* us to slice that little brat open! He *needs* innocent blood!"

"Don't believe everything you see in the movies, boy," said Lucifer. "I was a teacher, a bringer of light and knowledge. I believe in freedom and independence. What you're trying to do is take away another's right to live. And I can't allow that."

"Yeah…then let's sacrifice *you* instead!"

Dave swung the knife wildly on his quick approach. Lucifer evaded each attempted slash with grace and poise, until he finally reached a hand out and grabbed hold of Dave's wrist. Lucifer twisted the young man's arm behind his back pushing up until the knife fell from his fingers and hit the marble floor.

But Lucifer didn't stop there. Even with the knife out of the way, he still continued to apply pressure to the arm. Dave's screams grew louder, echoing in the chapel until they were deafened by a loud *crack*. He slumped to the ground, weeping at the pain in his broken arm.

Lucifer stepped back from Dave and Brock tried to attack him from behind. It was a sloppy attack and Lucifer could sense it coming. He grabbed Brock's arm and flipped him over, dropping him hard onto one of the benches.

Without a word, Lucifer approached the podium and

examined the grimoire. It was real, all right. Real and powerful. Even an idiot like these three could accidentally unleash something terrible with a book such as this. But as Lucifer tried to get a read off it, he found he was blocked. He couldn't see where the book came from or how Caitlin had managed to possess it. That would be a mystery he'd have to unravel later. For now, he closed the book and took it from the podium.

Lucifer knelt down beside the boy, who had fear in his eyes. The Morningstar offered a reassuring smile and the yellow of his eyes dimmed. Gently, he peeled the tape off the boy's mouth.

"Your name is Anthony, right?" asked Lucifer in a soft voice.

The boy nodded.

"Anthony, my name is…" he paused and then said, "Luc."

"Y'mean…like Luke Skywalker?"

Lucifer gave a tiny chuckle. "Yes, exactly like Luke Skywalker. Remember what he said to Princess Leia?"

"'I'm here to rescue you'?"

"That's correct, and that's why I'm here, too."

"So…you're like…a Jedi?"

"Something like that. Now let's get you out of here."

Lucifer removed the bindings and helped Anthony to his feet. He walked the boy to the door leading back into the main hall. With a snap of his finger, he created a small, floating orb of light that moved a few feet in front of them.

"I want you to follow the light to the front entrance. And then wait there for me."

"But it's dark. Aren't there ghosts in the cemetery at night?"

"No, Anthony. I promise you, no ghosts will harm you. I'll just be a moment. Just stay near the light and it will protect you."

Anthony gave a somewhat-apprehensive nod, then followed the light out back. Once he was out of earshot, Lucifer turned back to the three would-be demon worshippers.

"As a rule I generally don't like to lie, particularly not to an impressionable young child like that," said Lucifer. "But I didn't want him to be scared. Because you see, there actually *are* ghosts in this cemetery. Some quite famous ones, too."

Lucifer held out his arms to the side and begun muttering an incantation in the demonic language of Dimoori Sheol. Feathered wings emerged from his back and raised him off the ground and his eyes had the fiery intensity of a blazing inferno. All three of them could feel a sudden chill, as if the entire room was plunged into winter. As Lucifer continued the incantation, his voice boomed and echoed, like several people speaking all at once.

Once he finished, the wings retracted and his feet touched the marble floor. He turned his back on the three and then stepped out of the chapel.

"Enjoy your evening."

Lucifer snapped his fingers and the chapel doors closed, locking the three inside. As he strolled through the hall towards the entrance to the mausoleum, their screams followed him.

CHAPTER 2

L ouis Jordan's heart strained to pump more blood through his veins as he ran through the streets of Metairie, a residential neighborhood just outside of New Orleans. At forty-five and with a diet that primarily consisted of fast food, sugary soda, and frozen dinners, he wasn't the type to be going on a late-night run.

And his body punished him for it. Louis almost collapsed as he took refuge on one side of a department store, breathing so hard that it was almost painful. His stomach felt queasy and his head was dizzy. More than anything else, he just couldn't believe what he had seen as he was leaving the late-night drive-thru.

Couldn't be him... That was the thought echoing in Louis's mind ever since. But there he was—Philip Ranch, standing right in front of the car, bathed in the headlights. Before Louis could even register what he had seen, Phil began pounding on the hood of the car.

Louis had panicked and slammed his foot on the gas. He had then swerved out of the Wendy's lot and onto the street before skidding to a stop. As he was sitting there, he watched Phil's motionless body. Louis became curious and opened the door, hearing the *ping-ping* noise echoing from his car, warning him that the door was ajar.

The steps it had taken him to get closer to Phil were laborious. He had felt like some slow-motion replay on ESPN. That *ping-ping* sound was still the only thing Louis had heard, and its rhythm strangely seemed to match that of his own heart.

And then, Phil had jumped to his feet. That was when Louis began running.

He'd been running for ten minutes when he had almost collapsed. His hand clutched his chest through his short-sleeve button-down shirt, his tie rumpled and hanging loosely from his collar.

As he started to gain control over his breathing, he swallowed and peered around the edge of the store. The parking lot was quiet and he could see no sign of Phil. The shopping center was right along Canal No. 3 and the irony was that his condo was just across the canal.

But the closest way to cross it was by crossing on the overpass, which was an expressway. There was a bridge, but it was a little over half a mile further down the road. Not only did Louis not want to run that distance, but he was afraid that the longer he stayed out in the open, the quicker Phil could find him. That's why he was too scared to go back to the Wendy's to claim his car. Too much of a chance that Phil might see him.

Louis slowly moved from the side of the store. He walked towards the center of the empty parking lot and looked around. There was nothing unusual to be seen. His face was covered with a sheen of sweat that he wiped away with his hand. No sounds other than the occasional car driving along the boulevard.

Had no one else seen Phil? Was it all in Louis's

imagination? Was he simply going crazy? These were the questions that kept popping up in his mind and he had no real answers for them.

Louis walked slowly to the entrance of the shopping center and stared down both sides of the street. Again, everything seemed normal. But he also didn't want to take any chances. The canal wasn't that deep anyway, and late at night, he shouldn't have any problems crossing it without anyone noticing.

He'd go home, lock the door, then tomorrow, deal with the ramifications. His car would no doubt be towed, but at least he kept a spare key to his condo in his wallet just in case of emergencies.

Louis left the shopping center and walked as briskly as he could manage without straining himself. There were some other smaller shopping and business centers in this area and he went past them all until he finally came to a chainlink fence blocking his access to the canal. Louis reached up and grabbed hold of the links and pulled himself up.

Immediately he had started to regret that decision. Even though the fence wasn't very tall, it was still a lot harder to scale than he remembered back when he was a kid. And just as Louis reached the summit and was about to pull himself over, he heard a loud wail. It spooked him and he lost his grip, falling from the fence and landing on his back in the parking lot.

A face appeared in his line of sight—a police officer, his face concealed by the shadows cast from his hat.

"Mind tellin' me what you're doing?" asked the cop.

Louis sighed. *A cop, thank Christ almighty.* Now he'd be safe. Louis rolled over onto his stomach and then pushed himself up slowly to his feet. The cop took a few steps back, one hand resting on his nightstick, the other on his gun.

"Sorry, officer. I was just tryin' to get home."

The cop looked past the chainlink fence and across the canal. "You live over in those parts?"

Louis nodded.

"Y'know, there *are* easier ways to get to that part of town than scaling a fence and wading through a canal."

"You don't understand, Officer..." Louis stepped closer and squinted to read the name on the badge, "...Hudson. There's someone after me."

Hudson raised an incredulous eyebrow. He glanced over each shoulder and said, "I don't see anyone out here but you and me."

"I gave 'im the slip," said Louis. "But I'm afraid the longer I stay out here, the likelier it is that he finds me."

Hudson's hands remained on his belt, his head cocked to one side as he stared silently at Louis. "You been drinking tonight, sir?"

Louis shook his head. "Nossir. I was working late and was just on my way home. Stopped at the Wendy's to pick up something to eat and that's when he jumped outta nowhere."

"So that's *your* car out in the middle of Vets?" asked Hudson, jerking his thumb back towards the main road and referring to the thoroughfare by its local name.

Louis nodded. "I know I shouldn't have left it, but—"

Hudson stepped forward and cut him off. "Let me see your license."

"Right, of course."

Louis took his wallet from his back-pocket and handed his driver's license over to Hudson. The officer took it in one hand and drew his flashlight in the other, shining the beam over the tiny piece of plastic to read the information. He raised the beam up to Louis's face to confirm he matched the photo, then handed the license back.

"Mr. Jordan, I'm going to have to ask you to get back in your car and go home."

Louis's eyes widened. "No, you can't ask me to do that!"

"Fine, then consider it an order."

"You don't understand! He could be waiting there!"

Hudson sighed. "Mr. Jordan, I was just at your car. I got out of my cruiser to call it in as abandoned. Now you need to go pick it up before the tow gets here."

"Officer, please!" Louis clasped his hands together in a prayer-like pose, almost dropping to his knees to beg. "I can't go back there! Not tonight!"

"I can escort you—"

"Please, just let me go home!"

Hudson watched with confusion as Louis's eyes began visibly watering. It was clear that the man was possessed by some extreme fear. Maybe it was simple paranoia or maybe it was something more. Either way, Officer Hudson just knew that he wanted to get this guy out of his hair and there seemed to be a simple way to do that.

"Okay, I'll drive you home," he said. "That doesn't mean you're getting off here. The tow's gonna take your car at your expense. I *will* be writing you a citation for abandoning a vehicle in the middle of the road. Is that all understood?"

"Yes, yes, that's fine, thank you!"

Even though he'd only been a cop for five years, Hudson had never seen someone happy to get his car towed and be given a ticket. It was clear that he was well and truly scared. Hudson figured the best thing was to just get him home and then finish up his shift.

"Get in the back."

Louis did as he was ordered and almost rushed to climb into the back seat of the cruiser. Hudson made a quick radio call back to dispatch to update them on the situation, then got into the driver's seat and pulled away. He remembered Louis's address from the license and knew exactly where to go.

Hudson didn't ask any further questions about the strange circumstances of Louis's situation and Louis didn't offer up any information. The drive was a short one anyway, only about five minutes from the spot where Hudson had found Louis to Louis' condominium building.

Once Hudson pulled up to the building's entrance, he shifted the car into park and then began writing out the citation. He tore off a copy, then got out of the car, opened the rear door, and passed it to Louis.

"Thank you so much, Officer Hudson. I won't forget this, honest."

"Just make sure you pay that on time. And don't try to do any late-night fence-climbing again."

Louis nodded furiously, thanked Hudson a few more times, and then went inside the building. His unit was on the first floor and once inside, he quickly locked the door securely.

Leaning against the door, he could finally breathe a sigh of relief. It was over, the whole thing was over. Maybe it *was* just all in his head. Or maybe it was some crazy homeless guy who had wandered up to the Wendy's just as Louis was leaving, and Louis in his panic just *thought* it had been Phil.

Whatever the case, it was finished. Louis went to the kitchen and took out a bottle of beer for himself. He popped off the cap and walked over to his recliner near the large window and fell into it. Louis pulled off his tie and unbuttoned his collar, then sipped his beer and just savored the taste.

Crash!

The glass shattered inward and Louis screamed, jumping from the chair. A figure climbed through the broken window and now in artificial light of his living room, Louis got a very clear look at him.

He was dressed in a black suit and tie, but it was covered with dirt and mud with holes in several places. His flesh was rotting and pieces of it were missing, revealing gore and bone beneath. The eyes were wide open and bloodshot.

But even with all that horror, there was no mistake in Louis's mind that the thing he was staring at had once been Philip Ranch.

Louis backed away and he tripped over his coffee table, falling over and landing hard on it. The glass broke under his weight and he felt the pain in his back from striking the metal frame.

Phil lumbered closer, hovering right above Louis. He didn't say anything, just groaned as he reached his hands for Louis's face.

"Please, Phil! I'm sorry, I never wanted things to turn out the way they did!"

Louis's protests did nothing to deter the animated corpse that had once been Philip Ranch. And as the creature tore into Louis's flesh, Louis's screams rang out throughout the building, waking his neighbors and causing pets to howl in protest.

The police would be called, but by the time they arrived, they would find Louis Jordan an unrecognizable, bloody pulp, his flesh and limbs torn away. There would be no witnesses to the horrid crime.

And as for Philip Ranch? He would be gone by the time they arrived.

CHAPTER 3

When Lucifer arrived in Chicago, he had purchased a revitalized Tudor mansion in Evanston's Lakeshore Historic District. He had quickly furnished the place and stocked the library with books, plus other entertainment options including a smart TV and video games. The plan was for this to be his retirement home, where he could just enjoy himself now that he was no longer the ruler of Hell.

Things didn't quite work out that way. Long ago, Lucifer had realized that even in Hell, some laws had to be enforced. Mostly these laws involved violating the sovereignty of the different domains or the armistice with Heaven. And so, Lucifer used up a significant portion of his power to create Cocytus, a prison capable of holding the worst of the damned.

What Lucifer hadn't realized was that Cocytus's strength was tied in some form to Lucifer's own presence. And when he'd abdicated the throne and came to Earth, the prison's defenses were weakened, which enabled some of the more powerful prisoners to escape.

Lucifer had already dispatched one of them. Astaroth had been part of his rebellion against Heaven and was a true believer in the cause Lucifer had fought for. But after he'd attempted to interfere with Heaven's plans for the Nazarene, Lucifer was forced to imprison him in order to preserve the delicate peace. When he'd escaped, he had possessed a troubled young man, a man who was able to keep Astaroth imprisoned within his body and use the demonic power for vengeance.

That had been a few months ago. Yet Astaroth was just one of the escapees. The total number was unknown to Lucifer, but he had to find them all and destroy them. If Heaven became aware that Lucifer's abdication had enabled those escapes, they would see it as a violation of the armistice. And that would mean a fresh war between Heaven and Hell, one with Earth caught in the middle.

Lucifer had already seen firsthand the results of one war with Heaven. If there were another, he doubted much would be left standing once the dust settled. And so his retirement plans had been delayed for the time being, at least until he completed his mission.

But of course, finding the escapees was the difficult task. Astaroth had been drawn to Chicago by Lucifer's presence. And for the past few months, Lucifer had been following information and leads on cases of a more supernatural variety, provided by Detective Janice Wagner of the Chicago Police. All this was done in the hopes of finding other leads on the escapees.

Unfortunately, none had turned up. If Lucifer was in close enough proximity, he could sense their presence. Yet each of these jobs had turned up nothing useful, not even a lead on where the next escapee might have gone.

And so, he'd begun the task of exploring the internet. As he sat at a table beside the in-ground swimming pool, the umbrella overhead kept the summer afternoon sun off his face. He scrolled through message boards and websites devoted to the supernatural and the occult. These were hubs of information all around the world. If he was to learn anything about where his next target might be, this seemed the place to look.

"Can I get you a refill, my liege?"

Lucifer looked up with annoyance at the speaker. Belial was also a fallen angel who had been part of the rebellion against Heaven. The form he'd taken on Earth was of a tall, strongly built bald man. Though he despised Earth, he had dedicated himself to serving Lucifer and was even the one to inform the Morningstar of the escapes.

"How many times do I have to tell you?" asked Lucifer. "I'm no longer your liege or your lord or anything of that nature."

"Then how would you characterize our relationship?" asked Belial.

Lucifer leaned back in his chair and placed his arms on the rests. "Associates. Compatriots. Colleagues." He paused and then added, "Perhaps even friends?"

A low noise was produced in Belial's throat. He didn't seem too enthused by those options. "I'm not so sure I understand the point."

"And I shouldn't be surprised by that." Lucifer picked up the tumbler and finished the last of the scotch that was sitting at the bottom. He held the glass out to Belial. "I'm not fond of the whole master/servant relationship. But if you insist, I wouldn't mind a refill."

Belial took the glass. "Yes, si—" He stopped himself, the word 'sire' still on his mind. Without saying anything else, he simply turned and went into the house.

Lucifer sighed and returned his attention to his tablet. His finger swiped on the screen, reading through the posts on one of many occult forums he frequently checked. Nothing truly caught his attention, though. Mostly it was just the usual embellished stories heard from fourth- or fifth-hand sources.

Belial returned with the replenished scotch and set it in on the table. Lucifer thanked him and raised the glass to his lips, savoring that first sip of the alcohol.

"Have you made any progress?" asked Belial.

"Unfortunately no," said Lucifer. "We got lucky with Astaroth. But these other demons so far have seemed content to remain quiet. Bide their time, strengthen their power. Some may even never resurface."

"How would we find those?"

"That's a bridge we'll have to cross later. I'm more concerned in those with destructive tastes. And the longer they wait, the stronger they grow. That will make them all the more difficult to dispatch."

"Nothing from your allies?"

"Wagner has provided information on relevant cases, but none have really panned out. And Mara has agreed to tell me of any suspicious activity occurring within the supernatural underworld."

"What of..." Belial paused for a moment, "...the angel?

Lucifer could tell that just speaking her name angered Belial. The demon wasn't too fond of Heaven's choice to watch over the Morningstar's activities on Earth. And Belial had a right to be—there was a history between Lucifer and her, one that had ended in tears.

Anael.

The thought of her name summoned her image in his

mind. Her beautiful, pale face framed by dark tresses. The shimmering blue eyes that, though possessed by all angels, seemed somehow different in her. And an intellect and will that was strong enough to rival Lucifer's own.

After the Astaroth affair, they had left things on better terms than the last time they parted ways. But the fact remained that she was a servant of Heaven, bound to their will. And he was the Adversary, the great boogeyman used to scare willful little angels into following the rules.

"Anael said that she'd be…around."

"As your protector, should I be concerned by this?"

Lucifer grimaced. "You're not my protector, Belial. You do not work for me, you work *with* me and of your own volition."

"Then as your partner, should I be concerned?"

Lucifer didn't answer right away, just sipped his drink slowly. When he set it down on the table, he kept his fingers on the glass and stared at the gold liquid inside.

"I don't believe so," he said. "She's working under Uriel's command and he's a spineless sycophant if there ever was one. He knows his masters wouldn't risk moving against me. They don't want another war. And Uriel isn't as stupidly arrogant as Pyriel was. He wouldn't go against the Divine Choir's orders. Anael's job is to keep tabs on me and try to convince me to reclaim the throne."

"Perhaps another visit to the sorcerer then?"

Lucifer had considered that option. After all, he had helped uncover Astaroth's identity a few months ago. But Lucifer didn't quite trust that magician. He was something of an unpredictable sort and he'd also worked for Pyriel at one point.

"I'd rather not be any further indebted to Odysseus

Black." Lucifer looked at the tablet again. A new post had appeared and he hit the refresh button. "This seems interesting…"

"What is it?"

Lucifer clicked on the post and began reading the story of Louis Jordan. Many of the posts on here were local legends or outlandish conspiracy theories. But this one was not only recent, there were reputable sources backing up aspects of the story.

"Louis Jordan, middle-aged man from the New Orleans suburbs. He was found dead in his home a few days ago. His body was ripped to shreds. Neighbors heard him screaming and called the police. By the time they got there, the killer had escaped without a sight."

"How did the killer get in and out?"

"A window was broken."

Belial scoffed. "Forgive me, but I fail to see how this might be one of the fugitives. Seems like this was done by a human—a particularly savage human, I'll give you that. But human nonetheless."

"Sean Grady was human as well, and it's not as if his crimes would have been impossible without demonic involvement," said Lucifer. "But there's also something else. Apparently, earlier that night, Mr. Jordan was found by a police officer on patrol. The officer said Jordan seemed paranoid and refused to return to his car, which he'd abandoned in the middle of the road."

"So an insane human," said Belial. "I'm still not seeing anything about this that seems connected to our situation. Or even supernatural in the least."

"You may be right." Lucifer sighed. "It seems fairly thin, but there's something about it…I feel it's like an instinct…"

Lucifer leaned back in his chair and slowly sipped his drink. An idea started to form in his mind and he glanced up at Belial.

"Do we have all the ingredients we'd need for a summoning ritual?"

"Depends on what kind of summoning you're talking about."

"If we want to find out whether or not this is our kind of job, then perhaps we should start by speaking with Louis Jordan and learn just what exactly he was so scared of."

"Then we have everything we need, with the exception of one item," said Belial. "In order to summon Jordan's spirit—"

"We'd need one of his possessions. Right, of course," said Lucifer. "Fortunately, we have wings so we don't need any plane tickets."

"You want to go to New Orleans?" asked Belial.

"Are you telling me you don't?" Lucifer stood from the chair and strolled over to his partner. He patted him on the arm with a smile on his face. "Come on, Belial. The French Quarter, the music, the history. Let your hair down a little."

"…but I don't have any hair." Belial rubbed his bald head as if to prove his point.

Lucifer rolled his eyes. "Figuratively, my friend. We fly down to New Orleans, have a look around Jordan's home, and then summon his spirit. If everything seems on the level, then we'll return home and leave it at that. I'll even buy you dinner while we're down there."

Belial paused and considered the offer. "What sort of food does this New Orleans have?"

"You'll love it, trust me."

Lucifer returned to the table and closed up the tablet, then finished the rest of the scotch. He walked past Belial into the house.

"I'll have a quick jump in the shower, and then we'll fly down to the Big Easy."

Chicago served as one of the gateways for a place called Eden. It was just outside this plane of existence, known as an embassy of sorts between the angels of Heaven and the forces of Earth. Currently, it was managed by the angel Uriel. And Anael was one of his agents.

Uriel's predecessors had fashioned Eden into a kind of divine night club. It created a comfortable and inviting atmosphere for the humans who frequented the place. But for Anael, it felt stifling.

She didn't enjoy being on Earth, nor spending all her time here in Eden. But she had no choice other than to wait for something interesting to happen. Her job was a simple one—keep watch over the Adversary and find a way to get him to return to Hell.

Anael was perched on the terrace balustrade, looking over into the abyss below. As she stared into the darkness, some instinct suddenly struck her. There was something happening with the Adversary. She got the strong urge that she had to see just where he was going.

Anael stood upright on the balustrade and dove off the edge. Her wings extended and wrapped around her, and she vanished in a flash of azure light just before she was about to plunge into the darkness below.

CHAPTER 4

One of the features angels possessed—both those who had fallen and those who had not—was their wings. While these worked in the conventional manner, they also allowed for the ability to instantaneously travel from one point to another, regardless of how far apart. So while a commercial airliner would take over two hours to make the trip from Chicago to New Orleans, it was just the blink of an eye for Lucifer and Belial.

Before leaving Chicago, Lucifer had done some research to locate Louis Jordan's precise address. He and Belial then transported themselves to Metairie, just a few blocks away from the condominium building.

It had been a few days since Jordan's murder, so the media circus had left the building's other residents in peace. And as the pair strolled down the block towards the building's entrance, the only sign that something had occurred here was a wooden board hammered over a broken window in a first-floor unit.

Lucifer pointed at the wooden board. "I suppose that's the one we're looking for."

Belial said nothing. He had made his feelings on this matter clear, but Lucifer still had the gnawing suspicion this was something worth looking into. The pair went to the front door and entered the building's foyer. There were rows of mailboxes on each wall and a security door blocking their way into the building. Lucifer placed his hand on the knob and his eyes flickered. The door opened without incident.

Jordan's condo was near the entrance, and the door still had crime scene tape crisscrossing over its surface. Lucifer pulled the tape away without a second thought. Just as he'd done with the security door, all he needed to do was turn the knob and they were granted access to the unit.

The door led right into the kitchen and dining area. There was an empty pizza box on a small table just past the kitchen and some Chinese take-out containers. The sure sign of someone who didn't do much of their own cooking and likely lived alone.

Beyond the dining area was the living room. A TV in the corner near the broken window, a leather recliner beside the window, and a small loveseat with its back to them. There was shattered glass on the carpeted floor and the frame of a coffee table in front of the loveseat.

"Belial, do me a favor and explore the rest of the unit," said Lucifer. "Tell me if anything else seems out of sorts or if it's just here. And see if you can find some kind of personal possession."

"As you wish." Belial excused himself and walked down the adjoining hall to explore the bathroom and bedroom.

Lucifer knelt down by the remains of the coffee table. Tape in the outline of a body indicated where Jordan had been discovered, and the carpet had dried bloodstains in several spots. The off-white walls were also stained in a splatter pattern. Whatever had done this was truly vicious.

It certainly looked like an animal attack. Or something more.

He turned his head to the recliner and walked over to it. Lucifer touched the back cushion and felt a tingle, a brief flash. Next, he chose to sit in the chair completely, sinking into its leather cushions and resting his head against the back, his arms draped over the rests.

When the Morningstar closed his eyes, the memories came over him like a flood. In his mind, he was in the same position as Jordan had been, sitting in the chair and feeling a sense of relief. Sitting there in silence and slowly drinking a beer when all of a sudden, the brief peace was shattered—along with the window.

The next few images were scattered, in part by the panic Jordan had felt. And that panic was soon accompanied by pain as the…thing tore into his flesh. Lucifer's head jerked in short, rapid movements while he viewed the memories. He could feel the pain of flesh being ripped off his body, teeth biting into his neck, and he experienced the terror of dying. Jordan was screaming, but Lucifer couldn't decipher the words in the midst of all the other emotions.

Suddenly, Lucifer was pulled away from the vision. He opened his eyes and he was back in the present moment. Belial was bent over him, his arms on Lucifer's shoulders.

"I heard you scream," said Belial.

"You did?" asked Lucifer. His breath was short, his heart still pounding against his chest as he tried to push out the memory Jordan's panic and try and regain control over his body. "What did I say?"

"Nothing."

"Pity, I'd hoped there might be something useful in that."

"You saw something, didn't you?" asked Belial.

"Yes." Lucifer stood and turned, looking down at the chair. "It wasn't a human who did this. Well…at least it wasn't a human anymore."

"A demon?"

Lucifer shook his head. "No, it seemed to be a zombie. It broke through the window and attacked Jordan. He tripped as he tried to get away and fell on the coffee table. Then the zombie butchered him right here on the floor."

"Zombies don't act of their own accord," said Belial. "They're puppets under the control of a necromancer."

"And that necromancer could very well be one of our escapees," said Lucifer. "Did you find anything?"

"Nothing seemed disturbed."

"That doesn't surprise me. If Jordan was the zombie's only intended target, then it would have left once the task was complete."

"Where would it go?" asked Belial.

"Back to its grave or perhaps its master. Depends on whether the necromancer was finished with it. That's something else we should look into, though. See if any graves were disturbed recently. Did you find anything personal of his we can use in a summoning ritual?"

Belial reached in his pocket and pulled out a large, gold ring topped with a ruby. It had 1997 engraved into the side. "I found this."

Lucifer took it and once his fingers brushed the surface, he started to experience the memory of Louis's college graduation. "I think this will do nicely."

A knock came at the door. Lucifer and Belial exchanged glances of confusion. Lucifer walked towards the door, but Belial expressed an objection.

"Sire, shouldn't we simply leave?" he asked in a whispered voice.

Lucifer didn't answer and reached the door. He looked through the peephole and then turned back to Belial. "I think it's okay, just follow my lead." He opened the door and there was an old lady standing on the other side with gray hair tied into a bun, wearing thick glasses. She looked at him with uncertainty and curiosity.

"Good afternoon, ma'am. Is there something I can help you with?" asked Lucifer.

"Are…are you with the police?" she asked.

Lucifer gave a glance back at Belial's direction and then addressed the old lady again. "FBI, actually. We've been called in to consult on the case and decided we should have a look at the crime scene."

"Oh my. I'm sorry to disturb you, Agent…"

"…Starr," said Lucifer after a moment's pause. "Agent Luke Starr, at your service. And this is my partner, Agent… Ben Lyle."

He gestured at Belial, whose brow had perked up as his bottom lip protruded in disbelief.

"Oh, well it's certainly nice to meet you both. I hope you can find out what happened to pour Louie."

"Did you know him?" asked Lucifer.

"Why yes, of course. I'm Agnes Pemberton, I live just across the hall." She turned around and pointed to a unit with an open door.

"I would like to ask you some questions, if you have the time," said Lucifer.

"I'd certainly be happy to help you in any way I can. Would you like to follow me back to my place and I'll get you boys both a cup of coffee?"

"That sounds wonderful, Ms. Pemberton. Agent Lyle, shall we?"

Lucifer allowed Agnes to lead him across the hall and into her condo. Belial was a few paces behind him. The layout of her unit was the same as Jordan's, though obviously a very different decor. Agnes's place had a lot of framed photos on the wall, as well as mounted shelves containing a variety of knick-knacks. In contrast, Jordan's walls were mostly bare.

"Please, sit and make yourselves at home," said Agnes, gesturing to the plastic-covered couch.

Lucifer and Belial sat beside each other on the couch in front of the TV. A few moments later, Agnes came over carrying a tray with three cups of steaming coffee, a container of cream, and a small jar with a collection of sugar packets. Lucifer drank the coffee without any additions, while Belial grabbed a handful of about five sugar packets, tore them open at once, and emptied them into the cup.

"My, Agent Lyle. You certainly have a sweet tooth."

Belial grunted in response and sipped his coffee. Lucifer gave a nervous chuckle.

"Don't mind him, he's just a bit grumpy after air travel. We flew here from DC this morning," said Lucifer. "Now, you said you knew Jordan…?"

"Oh yes, such a dear man. Whenever I need help with something, Louie was always generous with his time. In fact, he put up those shelves for me."

"That's nice of him," said Lucifer. "Were you at home the night he died?"

Agnes gave a nod. "Yes, yes I was. I was having trouble sleeping, you see. At my age, I can only manage a few hours before I have to get up and use the ladies' room. And I couldn't get back to sleep, so I thought I'd watch some TV. And that was when I heard the scream. Scared the dickens out of me!"

Belial made a slurping sound as he sipped his coffee. Lucifer crossed his legs and leaned back into the couch, gently taking a drink from his own cup. Once Agnes finished, he leaned forward again and balanced the cup and saucer in his hand.

"Was it just a scream? Or did you hear him say something?"

"Oh, it's so hard to be sure. But it sounded like…yes, now that you mention it, it *did* seem like he was saying something?"

"That's interesting. And do you think you know what it was?"

"I think I heard him say the word…'fill.' And also what sounded like 'sorry.'"

"'Fill sorry'?" asked Lucifer.

"Could it have been a name?" asked Belial.

Agnes paused, her eyes rolling up in thought. "Y'know something, I think you might be right."

"Do you know if Mr. Jordan knew anyone named Phil?" asked Lucifer.

"Not that I'm aware of. But we didn't speak much about our personal lives. We were just neighbors."

"No one in the building you know of who goes by that name?" asked Lucifer.

Agnes hesitated for a moment, as if she was searching her memory. Then she said, "No, I don't believe so. I'm fairly active in the home owner's association here in the building, so I know pretty much everyone."

"Did he seem unusual at all in recent days?"

"He was coming home awfully late, I know that. I asked him once and he said he was really busy at work."

"And what kind of work does he do?"

"I think he was an investor of some sort, but I don't know much about his work. Except that he was quite successful. I'm honestly surprise he didn't buy a house or some fancy high-rise condo instead of living here. But he would always laugh and say he grew up in Metairie and he'd die here." Agnes's voice trailed off and she looked down as her bottom lip quivered slightly. "I suppose he was right about that…"

"Thank you for your time, Ms. Pemberton. We're both sorry for the loss of your friend."

"Do you have any clues? Do you think you can find whoever did this?" asked Agnes, looking up with glassy eyes.

"We'll do our best, I assure you," said Lucifer.

From there, they said their goodbyes and showed themselves out. Once they exited the building, Belial addressed his former master.

"'Agent Ben Lyle'…?" he asked.

"I was thinking on my feet. Couldn't very well have told her the truth, now could I?"

"What if she had asked for identification?"

"Simple glamour would have handled that."

Lucifer demonstrated by weaving a quick bit of magic to make it appear as if he was holding an FBI badge, complete with his photo and the name he'd given Agnes. He closed his hand and the badge dissipated.

"Now we have a name to go with our undead friend," said Lucifer.

"What about the spell?"

"We'll wait until the Witching Hour. Until then, how about a stroll through the cemetery?"

CHAPTER 5

Twice this week, Lucifer had found himself in a cemetery at night. First it was Rosehill in Chicago and now Metairie Cemetery named after the New Orleans suburb. He wondered if there was a chance that at some point, one of these hunts could lead him to a Tahitian beach.

He and Belial split up, moving through the rows of headstones. Even though it was night, they had no need for flashlights. One of the benefits of being supernatural beings was that they could see perfectly in dark as well as light. Lucifer had checked online and found Metairie had about fifty graves for Philip or Phillip and both he and Belial had split the list in two to check them all.

Lucifer was approaching the end of his list and so far hadn't found anything out of the ordinary. All the graves he'd seen were undisturbed and he wondered if perhaps this mysterious Phil had been buried in another location.

They could have simply waited until they had the opportunity to try summoning Louis's spirit, but Lucifer figured this would be one way to kill time until the Witching Hour approached.

"Lucifer!"

LUCIFER BOUND

When he heard Belial call his name, Lucifer stopped in his tracks and ran in the direction of the sound. He arrived and found Belial kneeling by the side of a grave. There was no grass on it and the lot stood out from the surrounding ones. Belial picked up some of the loose dirt and sifted it through his fingers.

"It's fresh," he said, then pointed at the headstone.

It was nothing more than a simple marker embedded in the ground with the name PHILIP RANCH engraved into the surface. Lucifer knelt down by the side and continued to read the information.

"Seems he and our friend Louis were around the same age, though Phil died five years ago," said Lucifer.

"What of the body?" asked Belial.

Lucifer placed both hands on the soft dirt and concentrated, reaching out with his senses. His eyes were like sparklers in the darkness. If the body were there, it would have a trace of the magicks used to animate it. But instead, Lucifer could feel nothing. He brushed off his hands and stood.

"No good," he said.

"Why was the grave filled if there's no corpse?" asked Belial.

"Perhaps Phil had no family to complain to, so the cemetery just quietly refilled it," said Lucifer. "No sense disturbing the locals if they don't need to. Now we just need to wait until the Witching Hour and we can ask Louis if he knows why a necromancer would want him dead."

"That's still several hours away."

"Then let's see about some food. You ever try jambalaya or gumbo?"

"I have no idea what any of those words mean."

Lucifer chuckled. "Then, my friend, you are in for a treat."

But as they started to walk away from the grave, they heard a muffled noise that sounded like a hand knocking on a wooden door. It was soon accompanied by other, similar sounds. Lucifer stopped and started to look around in the directions the noises came from. His eyes began smoldering in response and he sensed they would soon have company.

"Belial, get ready."

"Ready for wh—?"

Before Belial could even finish his question, the answer came in the form of a fist breaking through the ground. Belial fixed his attention on that spot as the corpse pulled itself from its grave. What remained of its skin was a pale yellow color. Its lips had already rotted away and only a single eye remained in a socket that no longer had any lids. It raced at him and Belial girded himself against the assault. The zombie's hands clawed at him, trying to break his flesh. Belial took hold of both its wrists and snapped them synchronously. The zombie gave no indication that it felt any pain and Belial grabbed its throat and then punched right through the skull.

That was just the first zombie to appear. Others quickly rose from their graves in the exact same manner. Lucifer watched as they surrounded the pair and willed his magic. His hands ignited with hellfire and he shaped it into the form of a flaming sword. Holding it in both hands, Lucifer slid into a stance and readied himself, burning eyes scanning the oncoming horde for the first one that would attack.

One came from the side and Lucifer turned to meet it. He severed its hands as it reached for him, then drove the sword up under its chin, piercing through the top of its head. When he retracted the blade, the fallen zombie collapsed on the ground. He pivoted just to see a zombie charging at him, trying to catch him unawares from behind. As Lucifer turned in that zombie's direction, the sword came with him and sliced right through its neck. The body's momentum carried it forward a few more steps before it stumbled and fell, the head landing right on top of it.

The different fighting styles of both Belial and Lucifer spoke to their personalitles. Lucifer preferred evasion and reliance on magic and hellfire. But though Belial had those abilities, he made little use of them. Instead he chose to rely on his brute demonic strength to tear through the zombies, leaving their ripped bodies to rot in scattered pieces across the grounds.

Belial tore the arm off one zombie and rammed its own jagged bone right through its eye. He pulled the head free and threw it like a shotput into the head of another zombie, the force of impact strong enough to liquefy both heads. A third came at him from behind and he delivered a back-kick right into its knee, breaking it so it bent backwards. Belial turned to face the zombie that was now on the ground and clapped both hands against the sides of its head, smashing the skull inwards.

Lucifer's sword transformed, going from one long sword to two shorter ones that he held in each hand. This allowed him to move with more mobility across the field, cutting through the zombies almost two or more at a time.

Even though he was truly a scholar at heart, angels were designed to be warriors. And Lucifer had to admit that he relished the chance to embrace that side of his heritage. He hadn't had a fight like this since The Fall, weaving through the ethereal planes to fight off the angels Michael and the Choir sent after him and his followers.

"It seems our necromancer knows about us," said Lucifer.

"How is it possible they figured it out so soon? We only just arrived!"

That was a good question. Perhaps it lent credence that the necromancer was another Cocytus escapee. Astaroth was able to sense Lucifer's presence, which was what drew him to Chicago in the first place. Now that Lucifer was in New Orleans, the demon must have sensed him in the same way.

Strange though that Lucifer was not yet able to do the same. For a moment, he wondered if this was another example of a spell being used to block his senses. Lucifer dismissed that idea almost as soon as it popped into his head. The spell used by Astaroth interfered with his psychometric abilities, but they were now working fine.

Lucifer impaled a nearby zombie and when he pulled the sword out, it changed its shape. The blade twisted and flowed, stretching out into what resembled a whip or a chain. He cracked it in the opposite direction and it snaked around a zombie's head. The smell of burning flesh filled the air and when Lucifer yanked on the end, the head snapped off. It rolled on the grass, now nothing more than a smoldering skull.

"How are they controlling this many?" asked Belial.

Lucifer had been wondering about that himself. Necromancy was a delicate art and very difficult to control. Even an experienced necromancer could have difficulty controlling more than one corpse at a time. But what they were witnessing here was dozens, and they were all fighting independent of each other. The power of this necromancer was vast. When Astaroth escaped, he was weak. But whoever they were dealing with was clearly the opposite.

"I think we may have to speed things up a bit. At the rate we're going, we'll be here all night," said Lucifer.

"What do you have in mind?"

"Something dramatic. But I'll need some time to prepare."

Belial groaned. He knew that meant he'd have to take on the horde single-handedly while Lucifer readied his spell.

"As you wish," he said and came to Lucifer's aid, drawing the attacking zombies' attention towards him.

Lucifer's wings flared into existence from his back and he rose up into the sky. Some of the zombies tried to grab him as he ascended, but he was able to make short work of them with hellfire. Once he was high enough, he placed his palms together and closed his eyes, concentrating.

One thing few knew was that the creation of Cocytus had greatly depleted the Morningstar's power. That in fact was one of the reasons for his self-imposed seclusion. Over the centuries, he had managed to recover quite a bit. But he had never been able to return to the height of his power when he first landed in Hell.

For most of the tasks, this wasn't much of a burden—teleportation, psychometry, supernatural senses, hellfire, and most kinds of spells were no trouble for him. But when it came to something like what he was about to do, the power needed was significant. And that meant he had to focus his magic and draw upon his soul's power.

It also meant he'd be left weak as a kitten once the dust settled.

Lucifer opened his eyes and they blazed like wild fires. He held his arms out to the sides and halos of golden energy appeared over his closed fists. In Heaven, Lucifer had the title of Lightbringer. It was one that held two meanings. The first referred to his knowledge and his work as a scholar to educate others.

The second was far more literal.

Lucifer's entire body burned like a second sun and he dropped towards the ground with incredible force and speed. He slammed right into the center of the horde and all that golden energy that had built up within him suddenly exploded in a radius across the horizon.

The zombies caught in the wave of light bent backwards and dropped to their knees. Rotted flesh was seared from their bones, leaving nothing more than blackened skeletons dotting the landscape. One by one, all their enemies fell, leaving Lucifer and Belial the only beings still alive in the cemetery.

Lucifer sat on one knee, his arms resting on the other, his head hung low. His breathing was labored and there were brief crackles of light as his body gave off steam. His wings fell weakly to the sides and slowly, they started to glow and recede into his back.

Belial was slow in his approach. He hadn't seen Lucifer expend that much power since the war. It had been awe-inspiring to watch then, just as it had been now. Once he reached Lucifer's side, he knelt down beside him.

"That was…" Belial didn't even have the words to describe what he'd just witnessed. "You did it."

Lucifer was still breathing hard, and he weakly raised

up his head. His eyes were not the same vibrant yellow Belial was used to—now they were far more pale. "Yes…I suppose I did…"

With those words, Lucifer's head began spinning. He felt an onset of lightness and his eyes rolled into the back of his head. He collapsed and Belial had to catch him to stop him from falling.

Belial gently cradled the Morningstar in his arms as he rose to a standing position. Yellow light emerged from Belial's back, and it shaped itself, taking on the form of crimson, bat-like wings. They extended outwards and wrapped around both the demon and the Morningstar. And in a flash of yellow light, the pair vanished.

CHAPTER 6

There was a large crowd of onlookers gathered around the entrance of the Metairie Cemetery when Sheriff Matthew Walsh pulled up to the gate. His officers had to try and clear a path for him and a barricade had been set up right outside the gate. Walsh parked his patrol car and climbed out just in time to be met by one of his deputies, Keith Fletcher.

"Thanks for coming down so quick, sir," said Fletcher.

Walsh glanced around at the gathered crowd. "Apparently not quick enough. How the hell did everyone hear about this so fast?"

"Seems someone posted some photos on Instagram from outside the fence. We had a bunch of people already wandering around inside the grounds by the time we arrived after getting the call. Had to herd 'em all out."

"Goddamn social media..." muttered Walsh. "Just another reason why this country's goin' down the crapper, Fletch."

"Yessir," his deputy agreed.

Walsh had lived in Metairie his entire life. He became a cop pretty much as soon as he graduated high school and then was eventually elected sheriff. In his twenty-five years on the force, he'd never seen anything like the sight that greeted him past the barricade and the cemetery gates.

Blackened skeletons littered the grounds, the flesh completely seared from their bones. From the looks of things, it seemed all of them had been residents of this cemetery, as the grounds were dotted by dug-up graves. Walsh took off his hat and scratched the bald part at the top of his head.

"What in the holy hell happened here?"

"Your guess is as good as ours, Sheriff," said Fletcher. "We got the call about an hour ago and came down here right away. Couldn't believe what we were seeing."

"And this all happened last night?"

"We got in touch with some of the cemetery personnel, they said everything was normal when they locked up yesterday afternoon."

Walsh shook his head as he knelt down by some of the skeletons. "That just isn't possible. There's gotta be a few dozen bodies here. Digging all those graves, taking them out, and then burning the flesh off 'em would take days."

"Like I said, your guess is as good as ours," Fletcher reiterated. "I've got some guys out there canvassing to see if anyone saw anything strange."

"Figures, the one time we actually *want* someone who was recording this shit on their phone…" muttered Walsh. He stood upright and just surveyed the cemetery. The whole thing seemed completely surreal.

"Got some reporters asking questions, too," said Fletcher.

"Tell 'em we're not ready to announce anything yet."

"Don't suppose you've got any theories, Sheriff?"

Walsh shot Fletcher a look that said, "don't be a fucking idiot," and that was all it took for Fletcher to shrink back and not say another word. Walsh began walking the grounds, moving past the forensics experts and other officers who were mumbling about what could have possibly caused all these skeletons to end up outside of their graves.

Some commotion momentarily drew Walsh's attention from the ghastly scene and over to the gate and the barricade. He saw a few of his deputies arguing with two people. This was something he could intervene in and possibly get something done. At the very least, it'd make him feel slightly less useless.

Walsh approached the deputies and took stock of the couple they were trying to turn away. Both were black and wearing sunglasses. One was an older man—tall and broad-shouldered, with very short hair that had spots of gray in it. He was dressed in a suit and Walsh imagined the man must've been sweating something fierce, though he exhibited no signs of discomfort. The other was a woman, young enough to be his daughter. She wore her long hair in braids that were tied back in a tail and her style of dress was more casual than her companion.

"What's goin' on here?" asked Walsh.

"These two are tryin' to get into the cemetery," said one of the deputies.

Walsh turned to the strangers. "This is an active police investigation." He pointed past the barricade. "I'm going to have to ask you to wait on the other side of that line."

"And you are…?" asked the man.

Walsh was taken aback by the man's attitude and pointed to the badge on his shirt. "I'm the damn sheriff of this town. You'd better show some respect, boy."

"As should you."

The man reached inside his jacket and the deputies

began to react. Walsh held up a hand in a gesture that told his men not to do anything rash. Last thing he needed was *more* attention.

The man produced a small wallet and flipped it open. It contained an FBI identification card and badge with the man's photo on it.

"Special Agent Isaiah Reeves," he said, then gestured to the woman. "This is my partner, Special Agent Samara Tillman."

As he said her name, Tillman produced a badge of her own. Walsh felt embarrassed by the revelation and gave his deputies the stink-eye for not asking who they were to begin with.

"You boys get back to minding the line," he said to the men. "I'll speak with the agents."

The deputies nodded sheepishly and went back to handling crowd control. As they left, Walsh felt both Reeves's and Tillman's eyes on him and he couldn't stop looking down at his polished shoes.

"Sorry about that," he finally said.

"Think nothing of it, Sheriff," said Reeves.

"How'd you get the call so fast?" asked Walsh. "I just found out about this myself."

"We've got our sources," said Reeves, offering nothing. "Would you mind if we had a look at what you've got?"

"Yeah, sure."

Walsh turned back to the gate and gestured for the agents to follow. He led them inside the cemetery and stood back to watch them. What surprised him the most was their total lack of surprise. Either they were very good at hiding their reactions or they had some experience with crazy on this level. He wasn't sure which he found more disturbing.

"This happened last night?" asked Tillman, the first words she spoke to Walsh.

"Yes, ma'am," said Walsh. "Cemetery staff said everything was kosher when they locked up for the day. Then sometime between then and sun-up…" Tillman moved away from Walsh before he could finish his sentence. "…this happened…?"

She walked among the bones and the open graves, her arms held down at her sides, but with her palms pointed towards the ground. Walsh gave his head a bewildering scratch as he watched her kneel down before one of the skeletons and slowly move her hands just above it. Her eyelids closed just slightly and she wasn't even really looking at the skeleton.

"Umm…Agent Reeves…is your parnter okay?"

"She's fine," said Reeves matter-of-factly. "Were there any witnesses? Anyone who saw what happened?"

"Not as of yet, but—" Walsh looked over his shoulder. "Hey Fletch! Come over here."

Fletcher left the deputy he was speaking to and came up to the sheriff and agent. "Yessir?"

"Any of those boys you sent out canvassing back yet?" asked Walsh.

"I'll go check." Fletcher walked away as he started speaking into his radio.

"Somethin' I don't get, Agent Reeves. Why would the FBI care about grave desecration in a New Orleans suburb?"

"I'm afraid that's privileged information, Sheriff," said Reeves without missing a beat. "Tell me, have there been any strange incidents in town lately?"

Walsh pursed his lips as he tried to think. "There was

a murder earlier this week, that's certainly unusual for us. Especially the way it was done."

"What happened?"

Walsh shrugged. "Someone broke into a guy's home and pretty much butchered him. Looked like a wild animal."

"And the victim?"

"Louis Jordan, a local guy."

Reeves gestured to the west end of the cemetery, which was bordered by homes. "Don't suppose he lived over in that area."

Walsh shook his head. "No, he was over near the edge of town as I recall."

"Any suspects?"

"Nah, we got nothing. Why? You think his death had some connection to this?"

Reeves said nothing. The silence made Walsh uncomfortable, so he was happy when they were interrupted by Fletcher with a deputy by his side.

"Sheriff?" asked Fletcher. "Parnell here just got back, wanted to let you know what he learned."

Walsh addressed the young deputy. "Go on, son. Agent Reeves here would like to hear what you have to say, too."

"I went around the homes on the west end over there, asked them if anyone saw anything," said Parnell. "Nobody saw anything directly, but a few said there was some sort of flash of bright light in the middle of the night. Woke some of 'em up."

"Did they say anything else about this light?" asked Reeves.

Parnell looked puzzled by the question. "N-not really, they just said it was like the sun had come up and then went back down."

"Isaiah?"

Reeves turned from the officers and looked in the direction of his partner. "Excuse me, gentlemen." He left them behind and walked over to Tillman, who stood from the skeleton. "You find anything?"

"This wasn't grave desecration, Zay. The seers were right, there's a necromancer at work in these parts," said Tillman.

Reeves always bristled slightly at the nickname his partner had chosen for him, but he'd largely come to accept it. "The sheriff said there was also a gruesome murder a few days ago. No suspects."

"Near the cemetery?"

Reeves shook his head. "No, but I think it's something we should investigate further. Could be a connection."

"Whatever the case, this is some major-league necromancy. Took someone with serious mojo to raise this many corpses at once."

"But why were they left this way?" asked Reeves. "Usually, a necromancer would have the corpse return to the grave or just drop it somewhere. Yet these look they've been seared."

"That's the other thing," said Tillman, then glanced around to make sure none of the local cops were listening in to their conversation. She took a step closer to Reeves and her voice became softer. "It's not just the necromancy I was able to pick up on. There was some *other* power here. Something ancient. Something...pure—I think."

Reeves's brow rose. "What does *that* mean?"

"I'm not sure. It's a power that feels pure, but also...I can't explain it. Not quite twisted...just...different. But whatever it is, it's *powerful*."

"Do you think you can track it?"

Tillman glanced down with a sigh. "Maybe, I don't know." She looked up at her partner and he noticed there was apprehension in her eyes. "Thing is, I'm not so sure this is something I want to cross paths with."

"You know we don't have a say in that sort of thing, Samara," said Reeves. "When you signed up with this outfit—"

"Yeah, yeah, I know…" she muttered. "I don't need to hear the speech again, okay?"

"Two powerful mystical signatures in the same place. Don't suppose that's coincidence."

"Well, it *is* New Orleans."

"Not something this big, though," said Reeves. "What do you think? They working together?"

"I'm not sure, maybe. But with this many corpses raised, think it's more likely they're at odds. Could mean we've got a potential ally?" asked Tillman.

"I want you to write this down, Agent—the enemy of your enemy is *not* necessarily your friend," said Reeves. "If these two are fighting each other, could very easily mean that they're both equal amounts of trouble."

"Can't blame a girl for being optimistic, Zay. Not everyone can pull off your cynicism."

"I'm not a cynic, I'm a realist," said Reeves. "Been doing this job long enough to know trouble when I smell it. And I'm getting a big dose of it in this place."

Tillman sucked in a deep breath and gave another glance around the cemetery. "Well, we're going to need *something* to tell these people. This incident's already drawn a big enough crowd and it's hit social media. If it starts trending, the guys upstairs won't be very happy."

"I know, I'll put in a call and see what sort of magic the boys in PR can come up with," said Reeves. "Meanwhile, I want you to start seeing what you have to do to find either this necromancer or whatever caused the light show that fried these corpses."

CHAPTER 7

Sunlight fell upon Lucifer's face and his eyelids fluttered. He groaned and rolled over, turning away from its brightness. Despite his best efforts, consciousness was returning and he opened his eyes. Lucifer pulled himself up to a sitting position and noticed he was in bed, draped in red, satin sheets. *His* sheets.

He climbed out of bed and set his feet on the carpeted floor. But as he stood, he started to stumble and managed to keep himself from falling by grabbing hold of the bedpost. Lucifer closed his eyes again, arms wrapped around the post, and tried to shake the mix of grogginess and vertigo from his head.

There was a knock on the closed door and Belial's voice came from the other side. "Sire…?"

"I told you…" Lucifer produced a guttural sound in his throat. "Never mind. Enter."

The door opened and Belial stepped inside. "I thought I heard you."

"Were you just standing outside the door?" asked Lucifer.

Belial nodded. "I've been awaiting your recovery. What you did in the cemetery seemed to take a lot out of you."

"Cemetery…?" Lucifer's grogginess was temporarily affecting his memory. He placed a hand against his forehead. The memory of unleashing the light on the zombies started to filter through his mind's eye. "Right, the cemetery. So why are we back in Chicago?"

"You passed out and I felt it was best to take you home where you could safely recover and gather your strength."

"How long was I out?"

"Two days."

Lucifer's ears perked up and his head snapped to attention. "I've been unconscious for two whole days?"

"As I said, it took a lot out of you."

"More than I'd expected…" Lucifer sat on the bed. Looking down at his legs, for the first time he realized he was dressed in silk pajamas. He inspected the black fabric as if it were the first time he'd seen it. "Did you…dress me?"

"I thought you would be more comfortable in your sleeping attire."

"So…you stripped my clothes off and put my pajamas on? While I was unconscious?"

"It seemed the thing to do. Was I wrong?"

"No, just a little weird is all." Lucifer took a breath and stretched his arms. "Damn, two days and yet I still feel exhausted."

"Perhaps some breakfast?" asked Belial.

"I don't feel up for cooking and I don't trust you in the kitchen," said Lucifer.

"I used to grill souls in the pits of Hell. I'm sure I can understand the basics of frying bacon."

"Thank you, but think I'd prefer ordering IHOP." Lucifer went for the smartphone on his bedside and opened up a delivery app. "Do you want anything?"

"No, I'm fine."

Lucifer shrugged. "Suit yourself." He put in his order and then set the phone back down. "I'm going to shower and then after breakfast, we can think about how we proceed with this necromancer."

There was apprehension in Belial's face. Lucifer studied the demon's wrinkling forehead and wavering eyes. He could read Belial's expression as if it were a flashing neon sign.

"You don't agree…?" he asked.

Belial wiped the uncertainty from his face. "No, it's… nothing. We can speak after you're refreshed. I'll go downstairs and wait for your delivery."

"Very well…" said Lucifer as Belial turned and closed the door. He took another try at standing. The dizziness was mostly gone now and he was able to remain stable on his feet. Some progress at least.

Lucifer entered the adjoining master bathroom and went to the wall-length mirror above the double-sink. After splashing some cold water on his face, Lucifer looked at his reflection in the mirror. He pulled down one of his eyelids and examined his eye up close. His irises were usually a bright, vibrant, almost-golden yellow. But now the color was very pale and dull, seemingly closer to gray. He chalked it up to his exhaustion, then stripped off his pajamas and climbed into the large shower unit.

The warm water hit his body and steam filled the unit, fogging up the glass. Lucifer worked his muscles, letting the heat and the water massage the fatigue from them. He hadn't attempted a display of power on that level since before the abddication and he'd underestimated just how depleted his powers now were.

He was in the shower for almost an hour, just enjoying the feel of the heat and steam. When he finished, Lucifer dressed in a pair of black slacks and a button-down burgundy shirt. He went downstairs into the dining room and saw Belial sitting at the table, his elbows perched on its surface and his hands clasped together. Lucifer's delivery was unpacked and set out for him at the head of the table.

He'd ordered the breakfast sampler, which consisted of eggs, sausage, ham, bacon, hashbrowns, and pancakes. Adding to that, Lucifer had also ordered a side of toast and biscuits, plus a plate of chicken and waffles. His long sleep combined with the fatigue he felt had given him a ravenous appetite and he dug into the food with relish, barely pausing to properly chew. The eggs, toast, and biscuits were the first to vanish, followed quickly by the pancakes and hashbrowns. He stopped eating from time to time just to take a drink of orange juice, draining the tall glass almost in seconds. Belial refilled the glass as Lucifer began working on the chicken and waffles.

It had only taken him about twenty minutes to devour all the food. Lucifer sat back in his chair, biting into the crispy bacon—the only thing left on the plate. He washed it down with some more juice as Belial just sat patiently waiting.

"You really should have ordered something," said Lucifer.

"I'm not as interested in food as you are, sir," said Belial. "How do you feel?"

"Content, but still drained. At least the hunger has been sated for now." Lucifer reached for the cup of hot coffee as a final element of his breakfast. "Now, we should discuss the situation in New Orleans. Have you done any work on the case since the cemetery?"

"Some." Belial picked up his own phone and brought up the newspaper article he'd saved. He passed the phone to Lucifer, who examined the headline—MASS GRAVE DESECRATION TRAUMATIZES TOWN. "Seems we drew some attention to ourselves."

"Certainly not ideal, I'll grant you that," said Lucifer. "But maybe that display of power will give our necromancer reason to come for us."

"Or they could go into hiding," said Belial.

"That's also a possibility."

The doorbell rang. Belial started to rise, but Lucifer gestured for him to remain seated.

"Continue monitoring the situation, see if any other strangeness falls upon Metairie," said Lucifer as he stood and went to the front door himself. "Let's just hope this little incident hasn't drawn any unwanted attention."

His mood had improved after breakfast, but when he saw the visitor who stood outside his front door, it soured once more. Her ebony hair spilled down her shoulders, contrasting with the white blazer she wore and her intense blue eyes had a disapproving nature to them.

"Speak of the devil…" muttered Lucifer as he walked from the door, leaving it open. "You might as well come in, Ana. Though I'm afraid I've already finished breakfast and now there's nothing left."

"I didn't come here for food," said Anael as she entered the house, closing the door behind her. "I know about New Orleans."

"Sire?" Belial came to the edge of the foyer. When he saw Anael, his eyes narrowed and his fingers curled into fists. "What are *you* doing here?"

"Relax, Belial. Everything's fine in here," said Lucifer.

"I don't trust any halos," said Belial.

"Just…go clean up the dishes. Please."

Belial grunted and left. Now that he and Anael were alone again, Lucifer moved on to the pressing question. "Have you been spying on me?"

"Not quite, more like monitoring your energy signature. Seeing if you did anything dramatic," said Anael. "First, your teleportation to New Orleans was curious. And then what you did in that cemetery…"

Lucifer walked into the adjoining sitting room and sat in the middle of one of the couches. He spread his arms out along the length of the back. "Is there a reason you're checking up on me?"

"I thought that would've been obvious after our last conversation." Anael followed him into the room but didn't sit. She folded her arms over her chest and stood tall in front of the sofa. "I told you I'd be keeping an eye on you, Adversary."

Lucifer bristled at that title. The fact that she continued her refusal to use his name still irked him. And she of course knew it, which was why she continued to do so.

"I'm doing the right thing, Ana. Tracking down and destroying some very dangerous damned souls."

"Souls that would still *be* imprisoned if not for *your* selfishness," said Anael.

Lucifer's lips tightened, but he kept his anger at bay. The last time he let his emotions get the better of him, it had ruined the progress he'd made with Anael. He wasn't about to do that again.

More than that, she was right. It *was* his fault and he

had been forced to accept that responsibility.

"You're right," he said. "But I'm trying to fix this. What more would you have me do?"

"My advice would be to let me and my people take care of these demons while you return to Hell," she said.

"You know that's not an option."

"Why?" She threw up an exasperated hand. "We have the power to take them down and you should be repairing Cocytus."

"I told you already that my powers aren't what they used to be. What I spent on constructing Cocytus weakened me to the point that I don't know if I *could* repair it."

"If you and the other Hell Lords combined your powers, you could in theory—"

"Beyond that, those souls have a tether of sorts to me. Only I'm capable of finding them. You'd lose precious time just trying to locate them and in that time, there's no telling how many more humans will die," said Lucifer. "Another issue is how the Divine Choir will react to this news. If they learn Cocytus was breached because of my abdication, they could view it as an act of war. They've been waiting for an excuse to shred the armistice."

Anael moved closer to him and her shoulders slumped. "Then we don't involve the Choir."

Lucifer's face contorted in a perplexed manner. "I'm sorry, could you repeat that?"

"We don't have to involve the Choir," she said once again. "I can assemble a squad of angels who are discrete. There's no reason for the Choir to know of any of this."

"I wouldn't trust any angel beyond you of keeping this secret," said Lucifer. "Possibly Gabriel or Rastiel, but they're both being closely watched after the nephilim affair."

"You're impossible." She shook her head. "So stubborn and arrogant that you can't accept when you're in over your—"

Anael suddenly silenced herself. Her mouth fell open and her entire body stiffened. Lucifer looked at her rounded eyes with curiosity, wondering just exactly was running through her head.

"Are you okay?" he asked.

She took an involuntary step back, still looking staggered. Then she moved closer, her eyes still locked on his, the surprise not leaving her face.

"Ana…?"

"Your…your power…"

"Oh, right," said Lucifer with a groan. "Yes, that power display in the cemetery left me weakened. But given time, I'm sure things will be back to normal."

"No…" Anael's head went from side to side, shaking in a slow, deliberate manner. "You don't understand. Lucifer…" She paused when she said his name, but then continued, "…your powers aren't weakened."

Lucifer leaned forward, resting his arms on his knees. "What are you trying to say, Ana?"

"Whatever you did…it's burned out your power. Your soul is…weak."

Lucifer looked down at his chest. "What?"

"Your powers are gone," she said. "You're *mortal*."

CHAPTER 8

The rented Nissan Sentra entered the parking lot of the Pine Woods Motel. Isaiah Reeves pulled into an empty spot right in front of his room, turned off the engine, and collected the takeout bags from the passenger seat. He unlocked the door to his room and walked inside. Once there, he quickly set the bags on the small wooden table and went to the door connecting his room to the adjoining one. The door was closed but not locked, so he opened it slowly and peeked inside.

"Samara…?" he asked.

The lights were off in Samara Tillman's room and the curtains drawn. He opened the door wide enough to enter and saw the flickering light of a candle in the darkness. Incense filled the room, and Isaiah saw his partner sitting cross-legged on the ground. A large piece of black cloth was laid out in front of her and she held her hands cupped close to her face, whispering something into them with her eyes closed. After she finished whispering, she tossed the contents of her hands onto the cloth.

It was a collection of tiny animal bones, shells, stones, and a few other little curios. After tossing them onto the cloth, Samara opened her eyes and leaned over. She careful-

61

ly examined each bone individually and also as an overall scene to try and divine what the spirits she was communing with had to say.

Isaiah knew better than to interrupt her during this process, so he went back into his room and closed the door behind him. He took off his jacket and tossed it on the queen-size bed, then grabbed one of the containers from the bags and sat on the edge. The box combo held a collection of chicken fingers and fries and he took one of the pieces of chicken and started to eat while he turned on the TV and scrolled through the available channels.

There wasn't much on. The local news had a brief segment about the cemetery but they were light on the details. Isaiah still wasn't sure how the organization would try to spin this, but that also wasn't his problem. All he had to do was find out what was happening in Metairie.

About twenty minutes came and went while he flipped through the channels. The food was good. There was some sauce that came with the chicken fingers, but Isaiah was content eating them as they were. He was pulled away from the TV when Samara opened the door and came inside.

"Brought you food," said Isaiah, nodding in the direction of the takeout bags on the table.

Samara walked over to the table and took a container. She sighed when she opened it. "We're right next to New Orleans, some of the best food in the world, and you pick up chicken fingers?"

"What's wrong with chicken fingers?"

She shook her head. "You've got the palette of an eight-year-old."

Isaiah shrugged. "Fine, next time I'll throw the bones and you can order food."

"Yeah, I wish. Problem is you don't know shit about divination, big guy."

"Then stop complaining and eat your chicken."

Samara chuckled and sat at the table. Isaiah turned off the TV and dropped the remote beside him on the bed. He turned slightly and looked in her direction.

"Did the bones tell you anything?" he asked.

Samara shook her head while chewing. She swallowed and followed up with, "The spirits aren't feeling very chatty today."

"Do we gotta sacrifice a goat or something?"

"Doesn't work that way. And besides, it's not that they're unable to talk."

"What, they giving you attitude?"

Samara shook her head. "No. It's weird, it feels like they're hesitating. Almost as if they're…" Her voice trailed off.

Isaiah watched her, waiting for her to continue. When she didn't, he tried prompting her by turning his wrist in circles. "As if they're what?"

"I don't know," she finally said. "Scared, I guess?"

Isaiah raised an eyebrow and bit into a fry. "You mean to tell me that somethin' in this town is *scaring* the ghosts?"

"I know how that sounds. Crazy, right?"

Isaiah shook his head. "Wasn't the word I was thinking. More like worrying. If something here is so bad, it's spooking things that normally do the spooking, that spells trouble in my book."

"On that we're agreed. But I don't think my rituals are going to be much help in this area," she said. "What about you?"

"Looked into that murder the sheriff mentioned. Surprising nobody, the Keystone Cops don't have any leads. So I went over to the building and spoke to some of his neighbors."

"And?"

Isaiah shook his head. "Not a whole lot. Though there was this one woman, his neighbor. Chatty old broad. Get this: she asked me why the FBI sent someone else around to talk to her."

That got Samara's attention and she turned away from the food to look at her partner. "Why's the FBI investigating a murder in a New Orleans suburb?"

"They aren't. I called it in just to be sure there weren't any wires crossed when we got sent down here," said Isaiah. "The lady said the two agents she spoke to were named Luke Starr and Ben Lyle. Bureau's never heard of either."

"So we've got some other players in town," said Samara. "Freelancers?"

"Maybe, maybe not. But I don't like the idea of interlopers mucking things up here. No telling what their intentions are."

"Could it be related to that other presence I felt in the cemetery?"

"I'd say it's a pretty good bet. But you know what the woman told me that I found really curious?"

Samara shook her head.

"She said the two agents both had what looked like yellow eyes."

Samara sucked in a breath. "So we've got demons in this town is what you're saying."

"At least two, possibly more. Who knows. But if they were behind that murder, they'd have no reason to question the old lady. The necromancy could be a different story, though. There's definitely some funky business going on here."

Samara finished off her food and took a long slurp of one of the accompanying sodas. She set the cup back down on the table, wiped her hands, and walked back to her room.

"Where are you going?" asked Isaiah.

"The spirits won't tell me about what went down in the cemetery. But maybe they'll have a thing or two to say about those demons."

Isaiah stood and followed her into the room. Samara lit the candle on the table and another stick of incense. She took the carefully wrapped cloth from the table and sat on the ground once more. She unfolded the cloth to reveal the bones gently resting in the center.

Isaiah wasn't really a big fan of magic. At the end of the day, he was basically just a cop doing a job. But in this line of work, the organization mandated that a mystical expert went along on all cases. And so he had been partnered up with Samara. She had been raised in the hoodoo tradition and had incorporated those beliefs and rituals with other forms of magic she'd studied at the academy.

It wasn't that Isaiah didn't believe in magic—he was in the wrong line of work if that had been the case. But he had trouble trusting in something that was so fluid and complex. Isaiah was raised in a typical Baptist household, then fell out of favor with religion when he served in the military. After what he'd seen in Iraq, he had trouble accepting the concept of a benevolent god. But his skills led to the organization recruiting him and then they showed him what was really out there.

Samara was still young. She'd only been working with

Isaiah for the past few years after things didn't end so well with Isaiah's previous partner. Fortunately, she was of a different sort and despite the difference in age and belief systems, Isaiah had no problems getting along with her. Over the course of time they had worked together, he came to view her as a little sister.

Samara went to the table and took a small squeeze bottle and a bowl. She sat back down and placed the bones in the bowl, then shook it a little. With the squeeze bottle, she dribbled a few drops of Florida Water onto the bones. Then she gathered them up and shook them in her hands. When she raised the bones up to her mouth, she gently breathed on them to warm them. Samara shook her hands again and Isaiah saw her lips moving.

"I know we just spoke, but I hope you don't mind if I ask you another question," she whispered. "It's asking a lot and for that I'm sorry. But I won't ask you about the cemetery. This time, I just want to know about some demons who have come to town. I'm hoping you can tell me anything you know about them?"

Isaiah knew the bone-throwing was just another form of divination and that it provded a way for Samara to commune with spirits. But any time he saw any of these rituals in action, he couldn't help the skeptic in him feeling like it was all ridiculous. He shouldn't—he'd seen plenty of crazy in his time with the organization to know that this stuff was very real.

Sometimes it got *too* real.

Samara tossed the bones on the cloth and started examining them. Isaiah moved closer and folded his arms over his broad chest. He looked down at the cloth as well to see if he could see even a little bit of what she saw. But from his perspective, it was nothing but a pile of tiny artifacts splayed out on a piece of cloth. He couldn't determine any sort of meaning or pattern from them.

He switched to observing his partner. Samara's face seemed to darken as she read over her bone set. Her eyes alternated in size, with her lids sometimes squinting and widening a moment later. Her lips moved imperceptibly, like she was trying to suss out the pronunciation of a difficult word she'd stumbled across.

Finally, she looked up from the bones at Isaiah and there was some concern in her face. She gathered up the bones and carefully wrapped them in the cloth, then stood. After placing the bones back on the table, she blew out the candle and turned on the room lights.

"You learn anything from that little experiment?" he asked.

"Yeah, and you're not gonna like it."

Samara went over to her bag and produced a bottle of rum she'd purchased when they got into town. She flipped over one of the motel glasses and poured some of the rum. While sipping the drink, she leaned against the wall. Sometimes a reading was hard on her and she needed something to take the edge off. This was clearly one of those times and Isaiah didn't want to push her too hard. She'd tell him once she was ready to. Once she'd had a chance to gather her bearings.

She finished the first glass and then poured herself a second. Halfway into drinking that one, she rubbed her eyes and looked up at her partner.

"The spirits didn't want to talk about the cemetery, but they were willing to say that two demons did in fact come to Metairie."

"Don't suppose they could tell you what sort of demons we're dealing with here," said Isaiah. He knew there were various types but that in general, it came down to two—the lower-level ones who needed to possess a body to walk around topside. And then there were the archdemons, who were powerful enough that they could assume a physical form without relying on possession.

"Archdemons of the worst kind," said Samara. "Zay… they're two of The Fallen."

Isaiah blinked a few times. The Fallen were the angels who were cast into Hell after the war. He'd heard of them but was fortunate to have never encountered any in his career.

"You're saying that we've got two fallen angels in town and they're *not* what the spirits are scared of?"

"Oh, it gets better." Samara tossed back the last of the rum and sat on the edge of her bed. "One of them is Lucifer himself."

Isaiah stood in silence for what felt like hours but was in reality just a few seconds.

"Sam, I think I'm gonna need some of that rum."

CHAPTER 9

I n his long existence, Lucifer had been down before. There were times when he thought he had been defeated, that he would never find a way out. But not once had he ever truly felt what it was to be powerless.

Until today.

Anael had just delivered that piece of information to him and he sunk back into his couch. His mouth hung loosely from his jaw and hadn't moved since she spoke. One could think it was fixed in that position. Almost ten minutes had passed since Anael's revelation and Lucifer hadn't spoken a word in that span. The silence was beginning to worry the angel. She looked away from him and then back.

"Lucifer…" It sounded strange for her to be using his name. For a very long time, even hearing it had upset her. Speaking it was almost entirely out of the question.

But these were strange times. And with this newfound vulnerability, perhaps some unconscious part of her wanted to reach out to him, to help him in some way.

Lucifer didn't acknowledge her when she spoke his name. He just continued to stare into space, distant and cut off from the rest of the world. But that wouldn't be acceptable. She had to find a way to bring him back.

"My wings…"

Lucifer's eyes moved when he spoke those words. He was back in the world, to at least some small extent. Though there was still a distance about him.

"What about them?" asked Anael.

"After you said…" Lucifer swallowed. "I've been trying to manifest them. I've been trying to summon up some spark of hellfire. Anything. But nothing's happened. Not even my wings will appear."

He locked his sight on her eyes.

"How is that possible, Anael?" he asked. "How could I be mortal?"

Anael opened her mouth to say something, but she had no words. Air simply passed through her lips but formed no sound. She sighed and closed her eyes, then gave a shake of her head.

"I don't know," she said. "For an angel to become mortal, it usually requires a powerful binding spell. But only an archangel could pull off something like that and you haven't seen any sigils on your body, have you?"

"No. And I doubt any angel would be fool enough to try something like that without Choir direction."

"Which the Choir is unlikely to have done given that it'd be seen as a direct breach of the armistice and lead to war," said Anael. "They want you back on Hell's throne, not trapped as a human."

"Then how did this happen?" Lucifer stood and started to walk around the room, his hand on his head as he tried to think over possibilities. "Our powers don't just disappear without any sort of cause."

"No, they don't…" Anael's eyes moved around the

room as she followed her train of thought. "But they aren't limitless."

Lucifer paused his pacing and shrugged. "Well no, of course not." He resumed his pacing. "But just because an athlete becomes exhausted doesn't mean he can never compete again. He just needs rest, and time, and—"

"And refueling." Anael's head perked up at that and she stood. "I think that's it."

Lucifer stopped and stared at her. "What? What did I miss?"

"Our powers come from the energy of our souls, but as we use them more, that energy is drained and needs replenishment, just as humans need replenishment through food."

"But we don't eat. At least not for the purposes of energy."

"Of course not, that isn't what I'm saying," said Anael. "Our respective dimensions, that's where our souls are recharged."

"Heaven and Hell," said Lucifer. "You're saying in order to recharge my powers…"

"You'd have to go back to Hell, precisely," said Anael.

Lucifer's eyes narrowed as he moved closer to her. His shoulders stiffened and each step he took was slow and deliberate. His chin curved towards his chest while he glared at her.

"This is a trick, isn't it?" he asked.

"What?"

"The Choir found some way to weaken me, and now that I'm powerless, they want me to believe the only way I can regain strength is by returning to Hell."

Anael shook her head. "No, that's not what's happening here."

"Don't lie to me!" Lucifer screamed at her. "My return to Hell is *exactly* what they want! You said so yourself!"

He lunged for her and grabbed her by the shoulders. Anael was surprised at his brashness, at how wild he'd grown in just a few short seconds. But she restrained herself from taking any action against him and to just allow him to flail about for the time being.

"Admit it!" he screamed. "Admit this is all some ploy!"

"Stop being so paranoid!" Anael shouted back.

"Were they responsible for New Orleans? Making me believe a necromancer was at work? Or perhaps they just hired one?" Lucifer began shaking her as he pelted her with accusations. "Maybe it was more than one. That thing at the cemetery, raising that many corpses at once required someone extremely powerful. Something that could only be attempted by—"

Anael's wings manifested from her back and her eyes burned with bright azure energy. A sudden discharge of soulfire from her hands threw Lucifer from her and she hovered above the floor, her wings stretching out to their full span.

"I've had enough of your recriminations, Adversary," she said in a hollow voice. "Once more you fail to take responsibility for your own actions. *You* broke your connection to Hell, *you* depleted your own power reserves, and you have no one to blame for your current predicament other than yourself."

Lucifer had been blown onto the ground in a small corner. The light from Anael's wings was blinding and he had to shield his eyes to protect them from the pain they felt.

"We did nothing to you. All of this is the result of your own hubris. Now, the choices you have are clear. You can either return to Hell and restore your power. Or you can stay here and wallow in self-pity. The choice is your—*ack!*"

Anael's words died abruptly. Even through the blue light, it was difficult to see. But as Lucifer attempted to look closely, he saw something like fire wrapped around her throat.

In a flash, Anael was yanked to the ground. Once she struck, the blue light began to fade. She was dragged across the floor, over to a spot where Belial stood, a hellfire lasso wrapped around his meaty arms.

"Seems I was right not to trust you," said Belial. "When I heard the raised voices, I came to see what was happening. Can't say I'm surprised to see that you'd use this visit as an opportunity to attack the Morningstar."

Anael's arm fell to one side and a soulfire sword quickly formed in her hand. She swung it up and severed the lasso. Her wings brought her off the ground and battered Belial in short order. Another burst of soulfire increased the distance between them.

"I've had enough of you as well, demon," she hissed.

Lucifer had gotten to his feet and started to approach her. Anael generated another sword and pointed it in his direction. Lucifer paused and just waited. She turned her gaze back to Belial, the other sword pointed at him. Her gaze went back and forth between the two as she spoke.

"Neither I, nor Heaven, nor any of its agents have anything to do with your current predicament," said Anael. "I came here because I was concerned for you. But it seems I was wrong to do so. Whatever this thing is, it's on you to deal with. If you can't settle this, then we'll have no choice but to intervene. And I promise you, that will *not* end well for you. You *know* what will happen if the Choir discovers this necromancer is one of yours."

Anael's weapons dissipated and she wrapped her wings around her body. The light's intensity filled the entire room and in a flash, she was gone.

Lucifer exhaled the breath he'd been holding. He walked back to his chair and sunk into it. Belial began straightening up anything that was knocked down or out of place by the scuffle.

"Good start for the day…" muttered Belial as he worked. "I *told* you I didn't trust her."

"Yes, and a gold star for you, my friend," said Lucifer.

Belial stood beside the chair and slid his hands into his pockets. "So what now?"

Lucifer propped his elbow on the armrest and rubbed his chin. "I think we have to return to New Orleans."

"You want to continue this search for the necromancer?"

"You heard Anael. If the Choir learns of this, it could lead to a cascade of dominos toppling. We don't want them to have any ammunition to use against us."

"Yes, that I understand. But without your powers…"

"Powerless doesn't equal helpless, Belial," said Lucifer. "I still know how to cast a spell. We can summon Louis Jordan's spirit if you help me."

"Very well. But wouldn't it be dangerous to return to New Orleans? If the necromancer can sense the spell, they could potentially track us."

"It's possible, but we don't have the luxury of choice.

The closer we are to where Jordan was killed, the easier the summoning will be to pull off. It's a risk, to be sure. Unfortunately without my powers to aid the spell, we need every advantage we can get. Provided you're still willing to assist."

"I remain at your service, Morningstar."

"Good, then we should start preparing. Hell only knows what else has happened since the cemetery." Lucifer glanced up at Belial. "I hope you don't mind providing the means of transport?"

"Of course, it will be my honor," said Belial.

"Then we should get started." Lucifer stood, but there was a kind of vacant look in his eyes.

"Are you okay?" asked Belial.

"I'd hoped things had improved with Anael. That maybe we could move past the things that were said and done before. But now…" Lucifer's voice softened and he closed his eyes. The silence lingered for a few moments before he opened his eyes again. "It's not important."

Belial was at a loss for the right words to say to his master in that moment. He wasn't one for relationships and he certainly didn't understand the affection the Morningstar still harbored for the angel. However, he could tell that Lucifer needed to hear something in that moment. And the only thing he could think of was to try to justify the paranoia that had driven a wedge between Lucifer and Anael.

"You might be right, though. This very well *could* be the machinations of the Choir. We still don't know if she was telling the truth."

"That's where we differ, Belial. I believe she *was.*" *And if I hadn't let my paranoia and arrogance get the better of me, perhaps we could have gotten her help.* That was the thought he chose not to vocalize. He could worry about Anael and what to do about his powers later. For now, he had to find a way to unearth the necromancer's identity and then figure out how he would kill them.

Once that job was done, though, Lucifer knew there would eventually come a reckoning between Anael and himself. He just didn't know how he would deal with it when that moment arrived.

CHAPTER 10

Ney Rey Park was a small park just behind Luthern High School. Even though it was after-hours and technically closed, the park currently had a few young occupants. Students from the high school who easily scaled the low chainlink fence and now lounged on the playground equipment.

Don Elwer opened up his backpack and pulled out the cans of Budweiser and passed them out to his four friends. They all opened their cans together and tapped them together before beginning to drink.

"What'd you have to promise to your brother for scoring these?" asked Shane, perhaps Don's closest friend since they were children.

"Gotta wash and vacuum his car before he drives back to school," said Don with a shrug. "Not the funnest gig, but whatever. At least he agreed to it. Normally he can be a dick about this sort of thing."

"Hey, he got us beer. Can't be that much of a dick," said Rich.

The three teenage boys continued joking and drinking. But of the two female members of the group, Annie noticed something wasn't quite right with Jenna. Rather than engaging with the others, she held her beer with both hands between her legs as she sat on the edge of the plastic slide. She wasn't even looking at them, just staring out into the distance.

"You okay, girl?" asked Annie.

Jenna seemed startled by the question. She glanced over at Annie and managed a sleight but forced smile, then looked back down at her beer.

"Jenna? What's wrong?" asked Annie again.

"Yeah, if you're not gonna drink that, I'll have it," said Rich.

"Sorry, I'm just…" Jenna's voice faded. She took a sip from the can and spoke again. "Are you sure we should be out here tonight?"

"Relax, nobody'll know we're here," said Shane. "Don and I have been sneaking out here for over a year and nobody's ever called the cops on us or nothing."

"No, I mean…that thing with the cemetery."

Don shrugged. "Some freak dug up some bodies. How's that our problem?"

"Yo, I heard it was some necrophile," said Rich.

Shane's brow furrowed. "Necrophile? The hell's that?"

"Y'know, someone who has a fetish for dead people."

"Bullshit!" said Shane. "You made that up."

"Hell no, man. It's a real thing," said Rich. "They dig up bodies and fuck 'em. In fact, I hear a lot of morticians are into that shit. Everybody knows but nobody does nothing because who the fuck else would do their job."

Annie rolled her eyes. "Could you stop being so gross?"

Rich held his hands up defensively. "What did I do? I was just talkin' facts."

"No, you're talking bullshit," said Shane. "Nobody's

fucking any dead people."

"The hell they ain't! I read all about it on the internet."

"Is this like that time you were convinced the queen was a blood-drinking lizard?"

Rich pointed in Shane's direction. "Y'know, fuck you, man. Because time's gonna tell on that one."

Shane chuckled and took another sip of his beer.

"Nobody had sex with those bodies. They were burned up or something," said Annie.

"Right, to destroy the DNA evidence. After the necrophiles come inside them, they gotta destroy the evidence. So they lit them all on fire."

"I don't think that's how any of that works…" Now Annie had been drawn into the conversation, too. So much so that she stopped paying attention to her friend and Jenna just went back to staring off into space.

Don had noticed however and moved from the picnic table he'd been sitting on. He walked over to the slide and leaned against it, looking down at Jenna. "Hey, don't let Rich get to you. He's just running his mouth off like usual."

Jenna gave a nod. "I know. I'm sorry, I know you went to a lot of trouble to get us booze an' all…"

Don shrugged. "No trouble at all. Like I said, my brother was pretty cool about buying for us this time."

"Yeah, I know. I just…I feel weird being out here."

"You wanna go for a walk?"

Jenna looked away and took another sip from her can. Then she stared at Don and nodded. "Uh-huh."

Don took a long drink from his can, keeping it turned upwards until he'd drained it of every last drop. He left the can on the picnic table next to his backpack. Jenna left hers on the gravel beneath the playground equipment and stood from the slide.

"Where are you guys goin'?" asked Annie.

"Just for a walk," said Don.

"Oh yeah, we know what that means." Rich made a circle with the thumb and index finger of one hand and then thrust the finger of the other hand in and out of the hole.

Annie slapped the back of his head. "I told you don't be gross."

"Damn, woman…" muttered Rich.

Don and Jenna walked side by side and the voices of their three friends faded into the distance. They approached the fence for the baseball diamond and Jenna pressed her back to it. Don leaned against it, stepping closer to her and looking down at her. From his vantage point, most of her face was hidden by her long blond hair. He brushed it behind her ear and she looked up at him.

"I'm glad you came out with us tonight," he said.

"Yeah, me too." Her smile was weak but genuine.

"That cemetery thing's really got you rattled, don't it?"

"My dad was buried there. His was one of the graves that was dug up," said Jenna.

Don's face drained of all color. "Oh shit, I'm sorry. I didn't know."

Jenna shook her head. "It's okay."

"And Rich…damn, I'll kick his ass later for what he said."

Jenna turned her body so it was facing Don and she placed a hand on his chest. "I said it's fine."

Don relaxed under her touch. He reached for the hand she had on his chest and wrapped his fingers around it. She didn't pull away and he stared at their hands as their fingers intertwined.

"Do they know anything?" he asked. "The cops, I mean."

"If they do, they ain't sayin'," said Jenna. "Just said it's an ongoing investigation and left it at that."

"So weird…" muttered Don. "But I'm sure they'll figure it out."

Jenna nodded, though it seemed she didn't quite believe it herself. Don had to doubt how much he believed his own words. Instead, he chose to change the subject and looked up at the night sky.

"Nice out tonight, huh?" he asked and then silently chided himself for such a stupid thing to say. But he wasn't quite sure how else to proceed with the conversation.

Jenna shrugged. "I guess."

Without even realizing it, she had moved closer to him. Don had noticed, however. He took his other hand and placed it on her hip. She didn't stop him, but now her head was tilted just slightly, looking up at him. Don brought his head down towards hers and their lips brushed together just for an instant.

They pulled away and Jenna looked at him with blue eyes. She smiled and he took that as a sign it was okay. He kissed her again, this time deeper. Jenna fell into the kiss and pressed her body against his, her arms wrapping around his neck.

The sudden rattling of the chainlink fence caused them to break the kiss. Jenna turned her head and hugged her body tighter to Don's as they both looked in the direction of the noise. Both of them were instantly afraid it was some adult who'd found them. Or even worse, the cops.

But what they saw was something that made them *wish* it had been a cop.

It was a corpse, its rotted flesh exposing gore, muscle, and bone. Decaying hands clutched the fence, pulling and pushing on it in a vain attempt to get through.

"What the *fuck* is that?" shouted Don. Jenna just screamed.

The screaming attracted the others, who ran over to see what the problem was. Upon seeing the zombie, Rich added his screaming to Jenna's. Shane threw the can at the fence.

"What the hell is *that* gonna do?" asked Annie.

Shane opened his mouth, said nothing, and just shrugged.

"Is that a goddamn fucking *zombie*?" screamed Rich as the corpse continued rattling the fence.

"Yeah, I think so," said Shane. "But don't worry, zombies are slow and stupid. Not like it's gonna get through that f—"

Shane cut himself off as the zombie began climbing the fence. It hopped over and landed in a crouch, then came running for them.

The five teenagers turned and ran from the zombie. It was able to move faster than any of them had expected. They tried to maintain some distance between themselves and the zombie, but it proved more difficult than they had imagined.

Rich stumbled and fell on the ground. The zombie pounced. His screams caused his friends to stop and turn. Rich tried in vain to fight off the corpse, but his efforts were wasted. He screamed for help, but his friends were all too paralyzed to do anything other than watch as the zombie tore into his flesh and devoured what it could.

They were frozen in place as they watched the grisly murder of their friend. Shane couldn't help it and bent over, throwing up the beer he'd consumed and the fast food he ate for dinner.

Rich's body no longer moved. The zombie looked up from its meal like a lion as it devoured a gazelle and licked its blood-splattered lips. It darted from Rich's corpse and came straight for them.

Don, Jenna, and Annie were able to make it over the fence. But Shane was still stunned from his vomiting episode and couldn't react as quickly. He had started to go up the fence, but just as he had reached the top, the zombie grabbed hold of his leg. Decaying teeth bit into his flesh and tore it from his calf. Shane screamed as he was pulled back down and then once more, the survivors could only watch as another of their friends was consumed by an undead creature.

They continued running, screaming. A siren broke through the night and a squad car sped onto the street, coming to a stop. Deputy Fletcher emerged from the car and drew his weapon, aiming it at the three kids. They all froze and held their hands up in the air.

"Stop right there!" shouted Fletcher.

But then he saw the zombie scaling the fence and jump down, landing on Don. Annie and Jenna fled from Don's sides as he flailed with the zombie on top of him. It bit into his neck and he screamed. Fletcher tracked the zombie, trying to find a clear shot. He fired a warning shot and the zombie looked up at him. That was exactly the moment he needed.

Fletcher fired again, this time hitting the zombie in

the forehead. The impact knocked it off Don's back, who scurried away. Fletcher moved towards the zombie and squeezed the trigger, firing round after round into the decaying body until finally, his gun just clicked on an empty chamber.

He ejected the magazine and loaded a fresh one, then fired a few more rounds. The zombie had stopped moving, and Fletcher carefully tested it by kicking its leg. The threat seemed passed now, with the zombie's head now little more than a crimson stain on the sidewalk.

Fletcher holstered his gun and faced the three survivors. Jenna had her arms around Don, who was bleeding profusely from the neck.

"Let's get him to a hospital," said Fletcher. "And then, I want you kids to tell me just what the fuck happened here tonight."

CHAPTER 11

Since Belial had been to the home of the late Louis Jordan once before, this time there was no need to simply teleport nearby. Instead, he could teleport directly inside the apartment with Lucifer in tow.

The yellow flash of light signaled their arrival and Belial's demonic wings folded back, sliding away from the Morningstar's body. The wings continued to glow with that unholy light as they became incorporeal and receded into Belial's back.

Lucifer didn't feel quite so comfortable being escorted around by Belial. But without his own powers, he had no choice. He'd never felt so helpless in all his existence, not even after The Fall. But he had to push forward and find the solution to this problem before it got worse.

The condo seemed untouched since their visit here a few days prior. The taped outline where Jordan died remained and even the empty takeout boxes still littered the kitchen. The unit was owned by Jordan so until his next of kin came around to lay claim, there was nothing anyone could do.

That suited their purposes just fine. Meant no real

chance of anyone barging in unexpected as Lucifer conducted his ritual.

He knelt down beside the outline and set the bag he carried on the floor in front of him. Lucifer opened the bag and took a can of red spraypaint. He removed the cap and shook the can, then sprayed a circle in front of him. Within the circle, he drew an Enochian sigil, one that represented the duality between life and death.

Out of the corner of his eye, Lucifer noticed Belial turn away as the sigil was drawn. Enochian was the language of the angels and Belial clearly resented his origins as one of them himself. Most demons did—in fact, some had even managed to forget they had once been servants of Heaven. Lucifer didn't favor such delusions. And as his original wings had remained even after his damnation, he couldn't entertain them even if he wanted to.

With the sigil complete, Lucifer returned the can to his bag. He next took out five large, black candles and set them at different points of the circle. One by one, he lit them with a long-stemmed lighter. In the center of the sigil, he placed Louis's class ring that they'd found on their last visit. Now finished, he rose to his feet to inspect his handiwork. With a satisfied nod, he summoned Belial for the next part.

"Kneel in front of the sigil," said Lucifer and Belial did so. Lucifer positioned himself behind the demon and placed his hands on Belial's head. "Take in the form of the sigil, commit it to memory so you see it just as clearly in your mind as you see it now."

There was a grumble—no doubt from having to stare at Enochian—but then Belial said, "Done."

"Good. Now close your eyes and against the dark,

I want you to see nothing other than the red sigil," said Lucifer.

Belial's eyelids slid down. There was a moment's pause and then he told Lucifer he was ready.

"Concentrate on the sigil. Imagine the energy flowing from inside your body and infusing the sigil with your essence."

Lucifer closed his own eyes. He could feel the power of Belial's soul beneath his hands, which meant it was beginning to work. Belial was prepped and ready, which meant the next part was again Lucifer's to play. The Morningstar began to utter an incantation in Enochian, a summoning spell that sought to reach beyond the veil and locate the spirit of the one who had perished in this home.

While Lucifer spoke the incantation, the air in the room dropped dramatically. He opened his eyes and could see the steam from his breath. The candles flickered and the sigil glowed bright orange like a hot coil.

In the center of the sigil, the air appeared distorted. Lucifer focused on that, still drawing on Belial's magical energy to try and enhance what he saw. The distortion took shape, becoming a translucent figure lying fetal within the circle.

Lucifer removed his hands from Belial's head and the demon opened his eyes and stood. The ghost of Louis Jordan looked up from the floor and was surprised at the two people he saw in front of him.

"Who are you?" he asked. "Where am I?"

"Are you Louis Jordan?" asked Lucifer.

The ghost nodded.

"You're in your condo, Louis."

"And who are you? Why are you here?" asked Louis.

"Do you remember what happened to you, Louis?" Lucifer was deliberate in constantly speaking the ghost's name. Crossing through the veil is not an easy proposition and spirits could and often did forget who they were. Constant reinforcement of their human identity helped prevent them from going insane and becoming vengeful.

"I…" Louis paused and looked down. He saw the sigil and his eyes widened in shock. "What's that thing on the floor? Why are there black candles? And what happened to my coffee table?"

"Think, Louis. Think about what happened to you. What's the last thing you remember?" asked Lucifer. "How did you feel?"

"I—I remember being scared…" said Louis.

"Good. And what were you scared of?"

"I was…running…from someone…"

"Who was it?"

"It…" Louis paused as he tried to search his memory. The disorientation from the summoning had obviously made it difficult to recall the details.

"Who were you running from? Was it a person?"

"Well…yeah, of course."

Lucifer remembered the name Philip Ranch from the cemetery and how Agnes had recalled hearing Louis shout the name Phil as he died. But Louis's current state meant it would be difficult to just confront him with that knowledge. Lucifer had to find a way to coax it out of him.

"Was it someone you knew?" asked Lucifer.

"Yeah…it was…" Louis's face looked pained at the memory. It seemed it wasn't so much that he *couldn't* remember, but more that he didn't *want* to remember.

"Tell me, Louis. It's important that I know who was after you."

"…Phil," said Louis. "Yeah, it was Phil Ranch. But… but that's not possible."

"Why isn't it possible?"

"Because Phil's dead. He died five years ago and…"

Louis's voice trailed off. Lucifer knelt down beside the sigil. He had to know more if he was going to find this necromancer.

"And what, Louis? What happened to Phil?"

Louis shook his head furiously. "No, I can't! I don't want to remember! Don't make me remember!"

"Louis, calm down. I'm your friend and I want to help you find out who did this. Why do you *not* want to remember what happened to Phil?"

"It wasn't my fault! It wasn't!"

Louis was growing more hysterical by the second. It was clear that whatever he remembered was too much for him to bear. Lucifer couldn't risk disturbing the spirit any further, not without potentially causing lasting damage to Louis's soul.

"Calm down, Louis. You don't have to think about Phil anymore," said Lucifer. "It's all over now, okay?"

"What is this?" asked Louis, looking down at his translucent hands. "What's wrong with my hands? How come I can see through them?" He looked up at Lucifer and Belial. "Who the hell are you people? What did you *do* to me?"

"I think you've had enough excitement for one day, Louis." Lucifer then began to speak a different incantation from the summoning ritual.

"What are you saying? What language is that?" asked Louis. "Tell me who you are!"

"If I told you, you'd just wish I hadn't," said Lucifer, then resumed the incantation. Once he finished, he nodded to Belial.

The demon swept his hand out and a gust of wind came out of nowhere, snuffing the candles' flames from existence. As the embers burned out, Louis's spirit faded into the ether as well, until there was no sign he was ever here.

"That wasn't much help," said Belial.

"On the contrary." Lucifer moved over to the couch and sat himself down, resting in the cushions. He looked up at Belial. "You heard the way he spoke about that man."

"I did, but what does that matter?"

"My guess is he feels guilt over Phil's death. Matbe even responsibility," said Lucifer. "Perhaps he killed him."

"When people come back from the dead to exact vengeance, it tends to be as spirits, not zombies," said Belial.

"Yes, you're right. Which means this necromancer might have some connection to Phil."

"Why would an escapee from Cocytus care about a human killing another human?"

"That's a very good question," said Lucifer. "And one I believe we should answer. But first—"

They were interrupted by a knocking at the door. Belial glanced over to the door and then at Lucifer. The Morningstar simply sighed. "Don't tell me it's that old woman again."

Belial went to the door and checked the peephole. He nodded at Lucifer. "It's her. Should we just leave?"

A thought entered Lucifer's head. One a bit unorthodox, but he decided to entertain it nonetheless. "Go outside and stall her, I'll be along in a minute."

"But—"

"And remember, you are Ben Lyle with the FBI," added Lucifer.

Belial look stunned by the command. Since time immemorial, he had never hesitated to follow one of Lucifer's orders. But the notion of dealing with a retired busybody somehow seemed the most frightening thing in the world to him.

"Go on, now," said Lucifer.

Belial sighed and opened the door and stepped out into the hallway. He closed the door behind him, but left it open just a crack. Lucifer could hear their voices as he gathered up the materials from the spell.

"Oh, well look who it is," she said. "Now, now, don't tell me, I never forget a name or a face…" Agnes clapped her hands after a pause. "Agent Lyle, right?"

"Umm, yes, that's correct," said Belial.

"It's good to see you again, Agent," said Agnes. "When that other fella was here, I thought maybe the FBI had switched you out. But now I see you're here."

"Right…we're still here. You know, investigating the… uh…the case…and…umm…"

Lucifer smiled to himself as he listened to Belial try and stumble his way through the conversation. He considered stepping into the hall so he could record this on his phone. The rest of The Fallen would no doubt have gotten more than a few laughs watching Belial, one of the most feared demons in Hell, struggling to make small talk with a little old lady.

But there was something in their conversation that gave Lucifer pause. As entertaining as this was, he had some questions for Agnes. He finished cleaning up and picked up the bag by its straps, then went to the door.

Lucifer joined them in the hallway and stood beside Belial. He smiled and tipped his head to Agnes.

"Ms. Pemberton, it's nice to see you again," he said.

"Oh, and Agent Stan," said Agnes with a wide smile.

"Starr, actually," said Lucifer.

Agnes's face flushed with a hint of crimson. "Oh dear me, please forgive me, Agent Starr. And after I just got through telling Agent Lyle here how good I am with names I go and embarrass myself like that. Couldn't you just die?"

"One would hope…" muttered Belial.

Lucifer gave Belial a quick and unnoticed kick to the shin.

"It's funny you should mention names, Ms. Pemberton. Because a name popped up in the investigation and we'd like to follow up on it. Tell me, have you ever heard of a Philip Ranch?"

"Ranch…?" asked Agnes, then shook her head. "No, I'm sorry, I can't say that I have, Agent."

"Ah. Well, it's probably nothing," said Lucifer. "And I'm sorry to have eavesdropped on your conversation with my partner, but you said something about the FBI sending another agent…?"

"Yes, that's correct. I think it was just yesterday there was another man here," said Agnes. "Tall, just like Agent Lyle. Though he was black." Agnes quickly corrected herself. "Now don't get it twisted, I don't think there's anything wrong with him being black."

"Of course you don't," said Lucifer.

"In fact, my youngest, Tiffany, she married a black. Very sweet boy."

Lucifer tried a gentle interruption. "Ms. Pemberton,

this other man, he said he was with the FBI?"

Agnes nodded.

"Did he give a name?" asked Lucifer.

"Yes, he did. It was…" she paused again, trying to think. "Agent Reeves! I remembered it because it reminded me of George Reeves. You remember, he played Superman on TV and—"

"I do remember," said Lucifer. "If you'll excuse me, I have to get going."

"Yes, it's time…for the report…to be…" Belial paused, trying to remember the word, "…reported."

"Oh, there's no rush, Agent Lyle," said Lucifer as he patted Belial on the shoulder.

"There's…not?" Belial looked at Lucifer, his eyes practically screaming for help.

"I can handle that on my own. I'm sure Ms. Pemberton would love to spend a few more minutes chatting," said Lucifer.

"But—"

"Now, Agent Lyle, you've been working yourself silly. And unless my nose is mistaken, Ms. Pemberton already has a pot of coffee ready to go, isn't that right?"

"Oh well of course. I'm always ready with coffee and sweets." Agnes took Belial's hand and started dragging him back towards her apartment.

Belial looked at Lucifer, his eyes still screaming for release. Lucifer just gave him a small wave and a smile.

"I'll see you later, Agent Lyle."

Lucifer went to the lobby of the building, chuckling as he did. It would do Belial some good to actually sit down and talk with a human one-on-one.

CHAPTER 12

Philip Ranch had committed suicide last year. Lucifer discovered the obituary through a search on his phone as he sat at the bar of a restaurant not far from the condo. He held the phone in one hand with a spoon in the other. While scrolling through the obituary, Lucifer fed himself a spoonful from the plate of jambalaya in front of him. The mix of andouille sausage, chicken, rice, and vegetables had just the right amount of spice.

It was interesting that he still felt hungry despite the large breakfast from the morning. Lucifer suspected it was some side-effect from the loss of his powers. His body was seeking out whatever nourishment it could find in order to try and replenish the lost energy. Though Lucifer suspected it would take a lot more than copious amounts of food to accomplish that.

For the time being, he was content to indulge his body's cravings. This kind of thing was the reason he chose to leave Hell in the first place, so he could enjoy the variety of experiences Earth and humanity had to offer. And he still intended to take advantage of those experiences, even if he had to do so while cleaning up his mess.

The interesting thing about Ranch was that he used to

be in business with Louis Jordan. The details were scarce in the obituary, however, and it just said that Ranch's fortunes had taken a tumble. Despondent and drowning in debt, Ranch apparently felt the only way out was to eat a bullet.

Jordan's fortunes, on the other hand, seemed to be perfectly fine. That could have been the reason for the guilt he felt, though—maybe Jordan screwed over his business partner. The suicide left Jordan feeling responsible. But Belial had been right—vengeance from beyond the grave was usually the domain of ghosts, not zombies. Zombies tended to be under the total control of the necromancer who raised them, unable to operate under independent thought or even any sort of instinct beyond feeding.

"So how did you manage to piss off a necromancer, Louis…?" muttered Lucifer as he washed down the jambalaya with a sip of beer.

Though his powers were gone, Lucifer still possessed some form of perception. It wasn't as strong as before, but he could at least get a feel for the environment. Particularly in close range. So Lucifer didn't even have to turn around in order to sense the mystic who now approached from behind.

The two stools on either side of him were pulled out and quickly occupied. Lucifer glanced around the rest of the bar and restaurant and saw that it was mostly empty. He took a napkin from the dispenser in front of him and wiped his mouth.

"I'm going to assume you didn't choose those particular seats due to a lack of options," he said.

"You'd assume correctly," said the man. He was middle-aged, broad-shouldered, with spots of gray in his black hair. "Just seemed like you were so lonely, sitting here all by yourself."

"I actually quite enjoy my solitude, thank you."

"That's no surprise," continued the man. "After all, I hear you've spent quite a long time living on your own."

Lucifer sat upright and took another drink from his beer. He regarded the man suspiciously out of the corner of his eyes. Whoever he was, he seemed more interested in doing the talking. But the woman who was with him and now sat to Lucifer's left was even more intriguing. She was younger than him but more than that, *she* was the mystic he'd sensed.

"And how would you know anything about my living arrangements?" asked Lucifer.

"Because I know who you are. And I'm not talking about 'Luke Starr,' the non-existent FBI agent you told that old lady you were," the man continued. "I'm talking another kind of star. Specifically the morning variety."

Lucifer smiled. "I see. And to whom might I be speaking? I can tell you're not an angel."

"Name's Isaiah Reeves."

"Ah yes, I'd heard about you from that same woman," said Lucifer. "For an FBI agent, you certainly seemed well-informed about my nature. And here I thought you g-men were more interested in conventional crimes as opposed to the supernatural variety."

Lucifer looked at the woman again. "Assuming, of course, that you actually *are* FBI. But I have my doubts on that score. Particularly where this one is concerned."

"What's that mean?" asked the woman.

"It means I can tell there's something special about you."

"Something tells me Samara isn't interested in your charms, Satan."

"That's a shame," said Lucifer. "How about you, Mr. Reeves?"

"*Agent* Reeves."

"No, I don't believe so," said Lucifer. "Now granted, I'm not completely well-versed in human law enforcement, but I certainly don't remember hearing anything about you boys investigating zombies and demons."

"Zay said we were agents, he never said anything to you about being FBI," said Samara.

"Then to whom exactly am I speaking?"

Isaiah looked around the room, presumably for any prying eyes and ears. Then he reached into his jacket and set down a closed wallet. Lucifer opened it and saw an ID card with Isaiah's name and picture. The other three-quarters of the ID were taken up by a large logo—a crossed crook and flail silhouette with an eye above them.

"Am I supposed to know what that means?" asked Lucifer.

"Office of Supernatural Investigation, Research and Intervention Specialists," said Isaiah. "Otherwise known as OSIRIS."

Lucifer smirked. "First rule of government funding: find a good acronym." He took another sip of his beer. "I wasn't aware that Uncle Sam knew much about the supernatural."

"You'd be surprised what Uncle Sam knows," said Samara. "Like the fact that the Devil is walking around a New Orleans suburb pretending to be an FBI agent."

"Agent Tillman over there knows a thing or two about magic herself," said Isaiah. "We got sent here because of that little thing in the cemetery. You know anything about that light show?"

"I might," said Lucifer.

"Well, that caught the attention of our bosses, so we got sent down here. And Samara did that thing where you talk with the spirits. What do you call it again?"

"Communing," said Samara.

"Right, she communed with the spirits," Isaiah continued. "They told us—well, told *her*—that the Devil himself was in town."

"And now, we were able to track you here," said Samara. "We weren't sure what we should do about you at first because…well, you're *Satan*. How are two agents supposed to take down evil incarnate?"

"That's actually a misconception, Agent Tillman," said Lucifer. "In point of fact, I'm not evil. Nor is there even any such thing as 'evil incarnate.' What I am is simply a scapegoat."

"And the King of Hell," said Isaiah.

"Retired, actually," said Lucifer. "Also, I never wanted nor cared much for the position in the first place."

"We were going to call in for some back-up once we figured out where you were. But turns out, there's something different about you," said Samara. "Seems you're not as powerful as the stories let on."

Isaiah reached beneath his coat and behind his back. He pulled something out and set it in front of Lucifer. They were iron handcuffs with runes engraved into the surface. The Morningstar recognized the markings as wards against magic.

"How about you put those on for us, then we'll take you back to a safe house we've got for a little chat?" asked

Isaiah. "And you can tell us all about why you're raising zombies in this town."

Lucifer chuckled. He pushed the handcuffs away and helped himself to more of the jambalaya.

"Did I say something funny?" asked Isaiah.

"Why yes, in point of fact, you did," said Lucifer after swallowing the mouthful of food. "I'm not responsible for the zombies, Agent Reeves. Instead—and I know how this is going to sound and how you'll react—we're on the same side."

Isaiah and Samara exchanged glances as Lucifer ate more of his lunch. He counted the seconds before the laughter started and the wait was about as long as he had expected—somewhere between two and three.

"You're telling us that Lucifer himself is trying to save lives?" asked Isaiah. "To protect the very souls he would normally love to torture for an eternity?"

Lucifer rolled his eyes. "More propaganda. Listen, I've never had any interest in torturing anyone. Hell is just a dimension I and my followers were banished to. Our only crime was wanting freedom from servitude."

"I'm sure it was," said Isaiah. "So why do you care about what happens in this town?"

"Because…" Lucifer took a breath and paused before he continued. This was going to be the part that proved difficult to explain. "One could make the argument… that I might have been…let's say, *indirectly* responsible for what's been happening in this town."

Isaiah and Samara once more had a silent conversation with their eyes. Then they each drew their guns and pointed them at Lucifer just as he was about to shovel another spoonful of food into his mouth. He sighed and set the spoon back down in the bowl.

"I don't suppose you could let me finish my lunch first?"

CHAPTER 13

Unfortunately, Lucifer didn't get the opportunity to finish his lunch. Instead, Isaiah put the handcuffs on him and the two OSIRIS agents drove Lucifer to a motel near the expressway. This seemed to be the safe house Isaiah had mentioned.

Once they pulled into one of the parking spots, Isaiah turned off the engine and grabbed Lucifer from the back seat. The handcuffs were unnecessary, but Lucifer didn't want them to know about his lack of power. But even if he had been able to use his abilities, the very existence of OSIRIS had sparked his curiosity. He wanted to know more about their organization—and hopefully find out if they'd learned any information he wasn't yet privy to.

Samara opened the motel room door and Isaiah, holding Lucifer by his arm, escorted the Devil inside. He pushed Lucifer onto the bed as he stepped back and drew his weapon. Samara closed the door behind her and leaned against it, folding her arms as she stared at Lucifer.

"Okay, time for you to start talking," said Isaiah. "And for your sake, I hope you've got a good story to tell."

"As you wish, Agent Reeves," Lucifer began. "You're right, I am the Devil. But that doesn't mean I'm some mustache-twirling supervillain. The truth of the matter is the rebellion I led against Heaven was more akin to your Revolutionary War. We wanted self-governance, away from the unquestioning servitude that Heaven demanded."

"You can spare us all that and jump straight to the zombies and how you're mixed up in all this," said Samara.

"Not a fan of backstory, are you? Fine, but you'll have to indulge me for just a bit," asked Lucifer. "After the war, my followers and I were cast down into Hell. By this point, humanity had started to spread all around the planet. They'd started to evolve, forming societies. Heaven wanted to control humanity and force them into the same role of servitude that the angels had been. I, of course, opposed this and had my followers try to oppose Heaven's machinations."

"How did that work out?" asked Isaiah.

"Not well. The newly transformed demons were still sore about their defeat and thought of the humans as playthings. The angels weren't much better. Soon enough, we started seeing offspring from the pairings of humans with celestials and that caused problems," said Lucifer. "These were known as the nephilim in the case of angel hybrids and the cambions were the demonic variety."

Isaiah pointed his gun with intention. "I swear, I'm about to shoot you in the face if you don't get to the damn point."

"The point is that these creatures were out of control. Cities burned, humans were slaughtered, and the forces of Heaven and Hell agreed to work together to bring them to heel," said Lucifer. "Once the dust had settled, both sides forged an armistice pact. A way to govern our interactions with the humans and each other and to police our own kind if they got out of hand."

"We see lots of demonic possessions every year. It's one of the reasons OSIRIS even exists. So I'd say you're not doing so hot on that policing," said Isaiah.

"The types of demons you encounter are usually human souls who have been corrupted by Hell. They're rogues who have escaped the pit and are generally not a huge threat," said Lucifer. "Think of them as shoplifters. Annoying, yes. But they aren't on the level of serial killers or terrorists."

"The last demon we went up against killed ten people before we exorcised him," said Samara.

"It's a metaphor, Agent Tillman. Though your point is taken, I could have chosen something better," said Lucifer. "In the cosmic scheme of things, these demons aren't a threat to the natural order. But when we did have ones that were, that's when my people stepped in. And these demons were imprisoned in a special place in Hell, called Cocytus."

"So you're saying whoever's responsible for these zombies is one of Hell's most-wanted?" asked Isaiah.

"Precisely," said Lucifer. "Unfortunately, my departure from Hell had an unexpected side-effect—it weakened the walls of Cocytus just enough so some of the more powerful prisoners were able to escape. I believe one such prisoner is responsible for what's been happening here in Metairie."

"And how do you know that?" asked Isaiah.

"All of Cocytus's prisoners are marked in the metaphysical sense. There's a certain feel to them. That was what I felt when I came to investigate what was happening here. What attracted your organization happened that night in the cemetery. A man had died and I was searching for information. That was when I was attacked by a number of freshly risen zombies and I had to rely on my powers to get me out of it."

"Let me see if I've put this together correctly." Samara placed her hands on her hips and moved from the door, coming closer to Lucifer. "You leave Hell, and because of that, your little prison is weakened. Now we've got a bunch of demons running around up here, including one who's raising zombies. And it's all because of you."

"More or less."

Samara looked up at Isaiah. "Sounds like a confession to me."

"If that were the case, but there's something the both of you are forgetting," said Lucifer. "I have no control over this or any other demon. If you take me into custody, it won't stop what's happening in Metairie. The demon will continue raising the dead to do his bidding, whatever that may be."

Isaiah still held his gun, but it was no longer pointed with the intention to shoot Lucifer as it was before. Lucifer stared at the seasoned agent, wondering if his words were getting through to him at all. The longer this went on, the more chance of damage being wrought. The Morningstar knew he had to escape this predicament and there seemed only one option.

"I can help you," he said. "I'm connected to the demon. The last one actually sought me out. This one may be interested in doing the same."

Samara scoffed. "We *hunt* demons. Exorcise them, kill them. We don't make deals with them."

"I'm no demon, Agent Tillman. Unlike the rest of The Fallen, I wasn't corrupted by Hell. I even still have my original wings."

"If you think we're stupid enough to fall for any of this bullshit, then I've got news for you—"

"Sam."

Isaiah's interruption was impactful. Samara stopped speaking and fixed her gaze on him. Lucifer watched the silent glances between the two. It was almost as if they were speaking a language just with those looks. He noted Samara's incredulity but also the stern eyes of Isaiah.

"Let's go outside for a minute," said Isaiah.

Samara didn't seem enthused by that. Her arms dropped to her sides and she moved quickly to the door, turning the knob and throwing it open before stepping outside the room. Isaiah turned his gaze back on Lucifer and gestured in the Morningstar's direction with his gun.

"Stay out of trouble, Lu," he said. "Because you're not leaving this room."

"That's fine, I've got time," said Lucifer. "Not as if there's a rogue, demonic necromancer on the loose…"

Isaiah joined Samara outside the motel room. He closed the door behind him and locked it, then reached into his jacket to take out a pack of cigarillos. Isaiah knew better than to offer one to Samara and he ignored the look of disgust on her face as he lit one.

"What the hell are you doing?" she asked.

"Having a smoke."

"You know what I mean."

Isaiah drew on the cigarillo before removing it from his mouth. The smoke exhaled from his nostrils and he leaned against the door.

"Do you know the biggest case I ever took on?" he asked.

"No, what?"

"Two demons working together to terrorize a family," he said. "That was it, just two pissant little demons looking to cause trouble."

Samara shrugged her shoulders. "Am I missing the point to this story?"

"Point is in all the time I've been doing this job, I've never dealt with something as big as this," said Isaiah. "We've got the Devil himself handcuffed in our motel room and we're looking for some archdemon necromancer."

"Am I hearing you right?" asked Samara before she pointed at the door. "You want to partner-up with Satan to solve this case?"

"Never said 'want,' but you tell me what other choices we're looking at here." Isaiah took another drag on the cigarillo. "Remember that we got another call this morning. Those kids who got attacked in the park. Whatever's happening here, it doesn't look like it's gonna stop. And if ol' Nick Scratch is offering to help us, well…"

Samara closed her eyes and clenched her fist. Isaiah knew she was trying to keep her anger from bursting out. Once she had successfully calmed herself, she let out a long breath and opened her eyes.

"I understand you're not a person of faith."

"Got nothin' to do with it."

"But I am. And you can't ask someone like me—someone who was raised in these beliefs—to just throw all that aside and partner with the very thing I've been told since birth is responsible for all the evil in the world."

"I know it's hard on you, and I'm not trying to diminish

that," said Isaiah. "But we don't live in a world of absolutes. To get the job done, that sometimes means you have to bite the bullet and work with people you despise."

"This isn't like working with some dark warlock or werewolf," said Samara. "We're talking about the Devil."

"You know what I can't stop thinking about?" asked Isaiah.

"What?"

"Nelson Mandela."

Samara blinked a few times, trying to make the connection. "I'm sorry…what?"

"Nelson Mandela was on terrorist watchlists until 2008. Even as president of South Africa, he had to apply for permission to enter the US and the State Department would only grant it on a case-by-case basis," said Isaiah. "The point is that old saying—one man's terrorist is another man's freedom fighter."

"You seriously did *not* just compare Mandela to Satan."

"Well, think about it." Isaiah moved his weight off the door and stepped towards the rental car. He sat on the hood while he smoked. "How much do we *really* know about Lucifer? What are the sources we have to consult? The Bible? The church? Isn't that kind of like asking Tom Cruise to give an objective assessment of L. Ron Hubbard?"

"There's also the demons that have been terrorizing mankind since before recorded history," said Samara.

"You heard what he said—they're basically criminals who managed to escape their prison," said Isaiah. "I'm just saying the world is full of gray areas. Why would we think celestial politics are simpler than human ones? If anything, I'd imagine they'd be even more complex."

"Zay, I love you but you're—"

Samara's entire body froze and her eyes widened. Isaiah stood from the hood of the car and stepped towards her.

"What is it?" he asked.

She drew her weapon and turned. But just as she did, some invisible force slammed into her body, tossing her aside. Isaiah drew his own gun and looked in different directions, trying to see who or what had attacked his partner. Before he could truly react, he too was thrown to the side.

A figure stepped forth from the shadows, approaching the motel door. He had long, dark hair and a goatee. With one solid kick, he threw the door off its hinges and entered the motel room.

Lucifer looked up from the bed and stared into the burning yellow eyes of the demon he had come to collect. The demon's hand burned with hellfire and he cut easily through the mystic restraints.

Before Lucifer could offer a single word, leathery, crimson wings emerged from the demon's back and wrapped around both him and Lucifer. And in a flash of yellow light, they were gone.

CHAPTER 14

For the second time that day, Lucifer found himself bound. Only this time it wasn't by handcuffs, but rather by a sigil drawn on the cement floor of wherever he'd been brought. The enclosure was a fixed cage outside. His kidnapper sat backwards on a chair right in front of him, an arm draped along the chair's back.

"Barbatos," said Lucifer. "I have to admit, you were not who I was expecting. Necromancy was never something you dabbled much in."

"Not originally, no," said Barbatos as he stood from the chair. "I was more charmed by the beasts of this world."

He walked over to the sole wall, which had no bars but a door. Barbatos opened the door and Lucifer heard a low gutteral sound. A quadruped entered the enclosure and Lucifer felt a chill go down his spine.

The creature was large, almost twelve feet in length. It had beautiful orange and white fur, with black stripes circling around its lean, muscular torso. Yellow eyes fixed on Lucifer and its tongue emerged to wet its lips.

Barbatos knelt beside the tiger and wrapped his arm around its neck. He started scratching under its chin and the tiger tossed its head back in contentment.

"So why the necromancy then?" asked Lucifer.

Barbatos looked away from his pet and back to his former master. "Because I'd seen what these humans have done and continue doing to this world and the beautiful creatures populating it. Do you know what this place we're in now was before I came around?"

"No, but I'm sure you're going to tell me."

"They had the nerve to call it an 'animal sanctuary' when it was anything but. The people running it treated the animals like garbage," said Barbatos. "Beaten and tortured and forced to perform for slack-jawed tourists. They didn't receive enough food and what they were given was spoiled. So, I commanded the animals to revolt."

"And the people?" asked Lucifer.

Barbatos grinned broadly. "Let's just say the tigers ate good that night."

"I'm still not seeing the connection between that and necromancy," said Lucifer.

Barbatos stood up from the tiger and sat back on the chair. "While the tigers had their fun, I examined the records the owner had kept. This place had a pair of investors—Philip Ranch and Louis Jordan. There were emails proving they knew what was happening here. I felt my work wasn't done."

"Then you learned Ranch was dead," said Lucifer.

Barbatos nodded. "Yeah. So I summoned his spirit, to see what I could learn about Jordan. The spirit told me how Jordan had screwed him out of a deal, how it had broken him and he took his own life. So I thought it was time for a little payback."

"And you raised Ranch's corpse," said Lucifer.

"That was going to be it, but then you and Belial came

to town." Barbatos chuckled. "You know, I wasn't even aware you'd left Hell. But I knew you were looking for me, and I had to try to get you off my trail. So I raised the corpses in the cemetery and sent them after you. I was going to leave it at that. Stay here in my little sanctuary with my new friends and enjoy my time here."

The tiger prowled around the enclosure, keeping its eyes on Lucifer and continuing to lick its lips in anticipation.

"But my curiosity got the better of me," said Barbatos. "So I made some inquiries, tried to learn why exactly the Morningstar was no longer ruling Hell. And that's how I learned about Astaroth."

"What does he have to do with any of this?"

Barbatos shook his head. "You don't seem to understand, do you? Astaroth had tried to turn Heaven's greatest weapon against them. And for that, you banished him to Cocytus. I wanted the animals to revolt against their human oppressors, and you locked me away, too. You've shown these people far more love and affection than you ever showed us, who backed you and your little war."

"Is that what this is all about, Barbatos?" asked Lucifer. "Simple revenge?"

"No, what happened to you in the cemetery, *that* was revenge," said Barbatos. "After learning about what you did to Astaroth and how you were now actually *helping* these talking monkeys, that made me realize there was only one way to truly see my magnificent beasts inherit what should have always been theirs. My problem before was I relied too much on the animals. But now, I've realized I can simply use my abilities to raise up the dead. Let humanity consume itself until there's nothing left, just as they consume everything else."

Barbatos chuckled and stood from the chair. He held out his arms in a gesture. "What do you think?"

"Well, as far as psychotic, genocidal plots go, it doesn't suck. So you have that going for you."

"The true genocide is what these mortals have been doing to this planet and its rightful inhabitants," said Barbatos. "This could be a world of wonder and beauty. Something beyond even Heaven itself. But they've turned it into a Hell for these creatures and even for themselves. Ninety percent of them suffer while ten percent live like kings. But they do nothing, just remain complacent in their misery. Better to show them mercy by eliminating them."

"An interesting philosophy, if not a wholly original one," said Lucifer. "But that stunt at the cemetery had to have taken a lot out of you. I doubt you have the power to pull off something like this on a global level."

"You're right, I don't," said Barbatos.

"You'll never be able to do it at this rate. The amount you kill would be a drop in the bucket compared to the new humans that are born to replace them," said Lucifer.

"You're absolutely right, my old king. That's why I have a plan far grander than you could imagine."

"A plan? You?" Lucifer gave a little smirk. "Now this I have to hear. Please, tell me all about this little ploy of yours and how it will work."

Barbatos chuckled. "I don't think so, Morningstar. I may have been trapped in Hell's prison for the past few centuries, but I still know not to spoil what's going to be a wonderful surprise."

The tiger stopped circling the cage. Its front legs bent down and its shoulders moved back, its rear end sticking up just slightly. The tiger never broke eye contact with Lucifer.

"I think your pet is feeling a little too playful for my tastes, Barbatos."

Barbatos stood from the chair and moved back into the corner of the enclosure. He smiled as he folded his arms over his chest. "I'm curious about testing out something."

With a snap of his fingers, the sigil dissipated. Not that it did Lucifer a whole lot of good. Sigil or no, he was still essentially mortal. And he wasn't looking forward to seeing how he'd stack up against a hungry tiger. But Barbatos wasn't giving him much of a choice in the matter.

Just as the tiger pounced, Lucifer lunged for the chair where Barbatos had been sitting. The tiger landed right where Lucifer had been standing and didn't waste a second in turning to face its prey. Lucifer held up the chair in an attempt to use it as a shield against the big cat.

The tiger roared and sprang once more. Lucifer held the chair out with his arms, trying to keep the tiger at bay. The animal's powerful claws cracked the wooden legs, breaking them off into splinters. Soon, there wouldn't be enough left of the chair to be much good as anything more than toothpicks.

The door was still open and that was the only chance Lucifer had. If he could get to the door and shut it, then he'd be able to hold the tiger back and find some way out of here.

Barbatos chuckled as he watched the tiger tear through Lucifer's defense. "He likes playing with you."

"Maybe he'd prefer playing with his savior?" asked Lucifer.

"Oh, we do. But we go at it a bit more rough," said Barbatos. "Though I'm wondering why you're just using the chair instead of something more effective. Like hellfire, for instance."

He knows, thought Lucifer. Just like Anael, Barbatos seemed capable of sensing that Lucifer had lost his powers. That only complicated matters, because any hope Lucifer had of somehow bluffing his way out of here was now gone.

As comical as it seemed, in that moment Lucifer couldn't help wondering just what would happen to his soul if that tiger killed him. Would he be sent back to Hell or would he go to Purgatory? Or would he just end up in some other place no one knew of? Perhaps remain trapped between dimensions like a spirit?

He had to get out of there. Lucifer pushed the chair into the tiger, which made the animal stand up on his hind legs. In that brief moment, Lucifer saw an opening and a chance to maybe get away. He slid forward and gave the tiger the hardest kick he could muster right in the cat's groin.

The tiger howled in pain and fell to the ground, stunned for the moment. Lucifer threw the chair at it and then ran for the door. Barbatos didn't seem to mind, just remained standing near the door with his arms folded, watching the scene play out.

Lucifer went through the door and pulled it shut. The tiger had recovered and now he ran towards Lucifer. Lucifer swung the heavy door shut and pushed against it as the tiger tried to get through. He used his arms and legs to try and keep the door shut long enough so it could be locked.

The door kept failing to close completely. Lucifer tried not to cringe at the ear-rending sound of the tiger's claws scraping against the metal. His lips curled back from gritted teeth as he pushed with all his strength.

It shut and he was able to slide the lock into place.

But even though the tiger was kept at bay, his impotent howls and attempts to claw through the door continued unabated.

Lucifer sighed and closed his eyes, taking a moment to just allow himself to breathe. He was very aware of just how lucky he was to escape that enclosure with his life. And now he had to find a way to get out of here. Then he'd have to learn just what exactly Barbatos's plan was.

But Lucifer's victory was short-lived. He heard a series of growls and he opened his eyes. The first tiger was just the tip of the iceberg, it seemed. Because while Lucifer had managed to escape that one, he was now in a larger enclosure with no less than three tigers. All of them moved from their seated positions and started taking deliberate steps in Lucifer's direction.

"I probably should have warned you. That door wasn't really an exit," said Barbatos, appearing beside Lucifer in a flash of yellow light. "But you have confirmed what I already suspected—the cemetery completely burned you out, didn't it?"

"You don't really want to see me mauled to death by tigers, do you?" asked Lucifer. "After everything we've been through?"

"What we've 'been through.'" Barbatos scoffed. "Tell me, Lucifer, what exactly was the highlight of our past together? When you convinced me to rebel against Heaven and thus be cast down into Hell? Or was it when you stabbed me in the back and imprisoned me within Cocytus?"

"That's a fair point..." muttered Lucifer. "But you're a sporting kind of demon, aren't you? What would be more entertaining—watching a powerless fallen angel get easily crushed by these glorious creatures, or giving him a fighting chance and the opportunity for a real show of power? Prove just how incredible your beasts truly are?"

"It's definitely a tempting proposition, I'll grant you that," said Barbatos. "But I think I'd much rather enjoy watching them tear you apart as you lie there helpless and screaming. You understand, don't you? After all, you left me helpless in that prison. So this would be pretty fitting payback."

The tigers moved in on Lucifer. And this time, he had no idea how he'd escape alive…

CHAPTER 15

E ach of the three tigers positioned themselves in a sort of semicircle around Lucifer, whose back was still to the wall. Behind the door, the tiger he'd managed to escape from still tried to futilely break through. Lucifer had read once that if facing a tiger or a bear, it was important not to run and not to show fear.

The phrase "easier said than done" suddenly seemed a gross understatement.

Barbatos's wings carried him off the ground and he hovered in the air with his arms folded and a perverted smile stretched across his face. He was going to make sure he enjoyed every single moment of Lucifer's demise.

"They like playing with their food before they eat, so I'm sure they'll have a great time with you," said Barbatos.

Lucifer thought about the chain of events that led him to this and how things might have turned out completely different had he not left Belial with Agnes. His logic was that Belial had very few interactions with humans since coming to Earth. And if he was going to remain by Lucifer's side, it was important he understood just why humanity was worth protecting against these demons.

Timing was never your strong suit, he thought to himself.

LUCIFER BOUND

If Belial had been around, the OSIRIS agents would never have managed to take Lucifer prisoner. And if Barbatos had been willing to attack while Belial was with Lucifer, it was unlikely things would play out in the same manner.

Lucifer shook those thoughts from his head. He kept falling back into old patterns of avoiding responsibility. But he knew it was his fault that his bodyguard hadn't been around to protect him and now he was paying the price for that error. It was Lucifer's fault he was powerless in the first place. These were the consequences of his own actions and he had to face up to them.

The first order of business was to get out of here. The tigers still kept their distance, just watching him. But Lucifer could see the growing impatience in their eyes. They were getting ready to strike and he had only seconds at best to figure out some sort of plan.

This enclosure was larger than the first and at the far end was the exit. In front and to the right of the exit was a pond and on the left side of the enclosure there stood a large tree. If he could get to the tree, he could climb to safety. But they would quickly surrounded it and just wait for him to try to come down, so he now reconsidered that idea.

He needed a distraction and his hand slowly moved into his pocket, his fingers taking hold of his cell phone. Lucifer slowly drew it out, keeping his movements very slow and deliberate so they didn't take it as an attack. He used his thumb to unlock the phone and held it by his side at an angle where he could just barely see the screen. Lucifer went into the phone's music app and hit shuffle on his playlist.

"There's some whores in this house, there's some whores in this house—"

"I said certified freak, seven days a week. Wet-ass pussy make that pull-out game weak, woo—"

Seemed Cardi B and Megan Thee Stallion were capable of not only drawing the ire of conservative media, but also distracting three hungry tigers. Because they all looked stunned by the music coming from the phone and Lucifer used that to his advantage, tossing the phone over to the tree.

The tigers went for the phone and Lucifer took his opportunity, trying to move as fast as he could towards the door without actually running. He looked up at Barbatos's scowling face and gave him a wink. Barbatos in response placed his thumb and index finger between his lips and let out a loud whistle. The tigers turned again and now their attention ws back on Lucifer.

"Dammit, I just *had* to gloat…"

The tigers were no longer patient. They charged from the tree, now standing between him and the exit with the pond right behind him. One of them rushed him and pounced. Lucifer braced himself, holding up his arms to try and protect his head.

The tiger slammed into him, knocking the two of them into the pond. The sudden shock of hitting the water had caused the tiger to lose his grip. Lucifer reached for the stone ledge and pulled himself out. But just as he was about to crawl from the pond, he felt a stinging pain as claws raked his back and tore his clothes.

Lucifer screamed but managed to deliver a strong kick right to the tiger's nose. The beast recoiled as Lucifer crawled on the stone-covered ground. The pain in his back made it hard to move, but he pushed himself to his feet nonetheless. Before he could take another step, the second tiger barreled into him. Lucifer's front torso was pinned up against the wall, the side of his face planting against the hard stone. He tried to pull away, but the tiger slashed him again.

The Morningstar hit the ground, landing on his back. His vision started to blur and he heard laughter coming from Barbatos. The last thing he saw were the heads of the three tigers poised above him, growling and snarling. He realized at that moment that this was the end. There was no way he could escape this time.

CHAPTER 16

After Belial had finally managed to get away from Agnes Pemberton, he'd gone to the restaurant where Lucifer went. But the demon was surprised to find that his king was not there. Though what he did sense was that Lucifer *had* been there. And also that there was another being who possessed magic abilities.

Belial had followed the trail, which led him to the motel where he found a man and a woman unconscious outside their motel room. The room itself had been broken into and a quick inspection of the room showed a pair of mangled iron handcuffs and a sigil on the door to prevent escape.

There was also a bag lying by the side of the bed. Belial opened it and saw the supplies Lucifer had used in the ritual to summon Jordan's spirit. The trail hadn't failed him, Lucifer had been here. And so had another. A name Belial hadn't heard in centuries. Not since he was sent to drag the demon back to Hell.

"Barbatos…"

Belial emerged from the room and looked at the two humans. He picked them both up and took them into the room. The one with the broken door adjoined another room, and the doors separating the two were open. Belial took them into that unit and closed the joining door behind him. He threw them each on the bed and waited.

It didn't take long before they woke with a start. And once they saw Belial and his glowing, yellow eyes, they quickly seemed to understand just who he was and the kind of predicament they'd found themselves.

"I'm only going to ask this once. If you humans make me repeat myself, then I'm going to become very cross," said Belial. "Who are you and where is the Morningstar?"

"I'm Samara Tillman and that's Isaiah Reeves," said the woman. "We're part of an organization that polices the supernatural."

"And the Morningstar?"

"He was with us, we took him into custody," said Samara.

Belial felt the rage beginning to boil inside him. "Why would you do something like that?"

"Because we had to," said Isaiah. "We were sent here to investigate the zombie problem and we found him. He admitted he was responsible for bringing that necromancer up here."

Belial shook his head. "You morons. The Morningstar is trying to *stop* the necromancer!"

"I'm sorry, and we're supposed to take the word of a demon that the Devil is doing the right thing?" asked Isaiah.

Belial moved closer and bent over. He brought his head in close so his face was inches away from Isaiah's. To the agent's credit, he didn't flinch in the slightest.

"Little human, if the mood struck me, I could force you to cut open your belly, remove your intestine, and use it as a jump-rope," said Belial. "The fact that I've given you the opportunity to explain yourself should speak volumes about my mercy. But even *I* have my limits."

"We were attacked," said Samara. "Someone who had power. Someone big."

Belial turned to look at Samara next. "Was it a demon?"

She sighed. "I don't know for sure. Everything happened so fast."

"You have power," said Belial. "I can sense it within you, so that means you would know."

Samara looked away for a brief moment, then stared Belial in the eyes. "Yes, I'm pretty sure it was."

"That's also what I sensed," said Belial. "We're on the same page."

"You knew, so why ask?"

"Confirmation. I do not rely on these senses often. And I also wanted to see how keen yours were," said Belial. "The demon is named Barbatos, I recognized his stench. A beastmaster of sorts. I detect a recent distortion in time and space, which means he teleported. Probably took Lucifer with him."

"Where are they?" asked Isaiah.

"I…do not know," said Belial, then looked to Samara. "But with her help, perhaps I can find out."

"You want *us* to help *you*?" asked Samara, standing from the bed.

"Precisely."

"Fuck off," said Isaiah. "No way in hell we're trusting a demon."

"Zay, hold up for a minute," said Samara.

"Hold up, my ass," said Isaiah, standing as well. "We know what these bastards are like. All three of them are probably working together."

"If we were, then I'd have no need of your assistance and you'd already be dead," said Belial.

"He's right. Look, we were sent here to take out this necromancer. And right now, this demon is the only lead we've got." Samara then added, "Besides, as I recall, you were willing to go along with Lucifer before. So what's changed?"

"Because it ended so well?" Isaiah sighed, scratched his beard, then walked over to the front door. "Fine, do what you have to. I'm off to go bribe the manager into keeping what went down here quiet."

Once Isaiah left the room, Samara faced Belial. "Okay, so what exactly do you need me to do?"

Belial held out his hands. "Take my hands, then close your eyes and focus your energies on the Morningstar. Think of nothing other than him."

"That's it?" asked Samara.

"Without his powers, it's difficult for me to sense him. But if I add your energies to mine, it just might work."

Samara took a deep breath then stepped forward. She reached out and linked hands with Belial. The two of them both closed their eyes and concentrated. A sensation passed through their hands, the feeling of energy moving between them, forming a kind of mystical circuit.

With the added power flowing through him, Belial was able to fix onto Lucifer's signature. But the distress he sensed was even worse. He could see flashes of Lucifer lying near-death, what remained of his energy fading quickly.

Belial broke the connection and stepped away from Samara. She was stunned by the sudden break and opened her eyes.

"What happened?"

"I have to go, he needs my help."

"Hey, we had a deal—!"

Belial wasted no more words. His wings emerged from his back and in the blink of an eye, he enveloped himself in them and teleported from the motel room.

In an instant, Belial now found himself in an enclosure of some kind. He looked up and saw Barbatos hovering above him. And what was more, he saw his master. Lucifer was on the ground with three tigers standing over him, beginning to tear into his flesh.

"No!"

Belial's hands burst with hellfire that he quickly forged into a lasso. He threw it around one of the tigers and pulled him off Lucifer. The other two tigers were distracted by the new arrival and turned from their fallen prey to see the new threat.

The tiger Belial had ensnared was thrown across the enclosure and slammed into the far wall. Belial then faced the other two and met their hunter's gaze. One pounced without waiting another second. Belial grabbed the tiger by his arms and spun him. The tiger was pinned to the ground by Belial's strength.

The third tiger just watched. Belial was ready to take him on as well, but this one seemed the smartest of the group. Rather than trying to engage Belial, he simply turned away and walked off into the corner where he laid down and began grooming himself.

Belial went to Lucifer's side and placed his hand on his master's chest. There was still some life within him, though not much. If Belial didn't act fast, the Morningstar would die.

"You shouldn't have come here," said Barbatos.

LUCIFER BOUND

Belial turned his own hunter's gaze up at the escaped demon. And under that gaze, Barbatos flinched.

"The last time I dragged your sorry ass back to Hell, it was just a mission," said Belial. "This time, you've harmed my master. I'd advise you not to make me any angrier than I already am."

Barbatos drew a sharp breath but said no words. Belial gently picked up Lucifer and his wings closed around the two of them. In a flash of light, they were gone.

CHAPTER 17

Belial sat at Lucifer's bedside, his elbows propped on his bent knees and his chin resting on his balled fists. He had taken Lucifer back to the Chicago estate where he stitched and bandaged the wounds to the best of his ability. But Lucifer hadn't yet regained consciousness. His pulse was weak and Belial didn't know how much more time he had.

What the Morningstar needed was a healer. And while Belial could be accused of many things, healer certainly wasn't one of them. As it were, he barely utilized any magic beyond hellfire. He wouldn't even know where to begin with a healing spell.

But if he did nothing, then there would only be one outcome—the Devil would die. Belial wasn't about to let that happen, though he didn't know who could provide help. Lucifer was the one who made the plans and had the connections. If their positions were reversed, he would have already found a solution.

Belial wasn't as smart and he knew it. He was just the muscle, here to support the man he'd looked up to for eons. The demon reached out for the Morningstar's limp hand and he gave it a gentle squeeze. It was a tender display of affection—and one Belial would deny to his dying breath had ever actually occurred.

"What am I supposed to do?" he asked in a whisper. Belial looked at Lucifer's face. His eyes remained closed and there wasn't the slightest hint of any reaction—not even a small twitch of a muscle.

Belial stood from the chair beside the bed and walked over to the windows. He'd opened the curtains out of some vain hope that being exposed to sunlight might help Lucifer wake sooner. It was utterly ridiculous, but Belial's options at that moment were few and far between.

His first thought was to reach out to Mara. But when he tried to contact her, he'd been told by one of her underlings that she was on a routine trip to Hell in order to report to Lilith. Odysseus Black was an option Belial had dismissed out of hand. The old sorcerer was powerful, but he was also as opportunistic as the day was long. There was no doubt in Belial's mind that Odysseus would try to exploit Lucifer's condition—both the need for a healer and lack of powers—to the fullest extent possible.

Belial propped his forearm against the window and touched his forehead to the glass. There *was* another option. But it was the one he despised the most. If he went there, they could easily turn him away before he'd said a single word. And *she* had made her intentions quite clear the last time they'd met.

The demon looked upon his master again. Belial approached the bed and knelt on one knee, then bowed his head. "Please, my Lord. Give me some sign of what I should do. I need your wisdom to guide me."

Of course, Lucifer didn't honor Belial's prayer. Had he been conscious, he would have chided Belial for even *thinking* such a thing. Lucifer didn't want praise or worship or magical thinking. He wanted others to make their own decisions. And that was the task Belial now had before him.

The demon rose. "If you can hear me, I apologize for that. I know you wouldn't approve. I just—" He stopped himself and then sighed. "I wish I was more like you. I wish I had your strength to live a life with the belief that I didn't need some guiding father figure. To live a life free of the constraints of faith…"

He laid a hand on Lucifer's shoulder.

"I'll return soon. You have my word, sire."

As Belial walked away from the bedside, his demonic wings emerged from his back. He took a breath, steeling himself for the task that lay ahead. And he wrapped himself in his wings. There was a bright, yellow light that for the briefest of moments illuminated the room, and then faded. And Belial along with it.

Belial rematerialized in an alley near the Willis Tower. His wings receded into his back and he emerged from the alley, walking towards the front entrance. He had never been here before—and even entering put not only his own life, but also Lucifer's and all of Hell at risk.

The emotion Belial felt as he walked into the lobby was unlike anything he had ever really known before—this was fear. He'd become well-accustomed to anger and hate, but fear was a new experience for him. Belial entered the elevator with a group of humans and stood near the back of the car as it began its ascent.

As the floors passed, the number of passengers decreased until Belial was the only one left. He stepped up to the elevator controls and stared at the empty spot above the buttons. Lucifer had told him the procedure and Belial never forgot anything. But he still hesitated, even going slower than he needed to as he used his finger to draw an invisible sigil on the console.

The air around where he'd traced his finger shimmered and distorted until a white button came into existence. Belial waited a moment and then hit the button with his palm. He stepped back and took a deep breath.

The elevator surged upward, feeling like a rocket shooting off into space. Belial's heart rate increased and he closed his eyes. He felt in the presence of something he hadn't experienced since The Fall—the presence of angels.

The elevator stopped and the doors opened, revealing a large, white area. There were people gathered about and as Belial emerged, he saw the design and architecture was not unlike an upscale piano bar. All the furniture was white, just as the walls, floor, and ceiling.

Eyes watched him as he moved through the club known as Eden. The people here were a mix—some angels, some other mystic beings, and also a few humans who either had connections or possessed their own supernatural powers. And almost all of them knew exactly what he was. Just as he could sense what they were, so too could they with him.

"What are *you* doing here?"

The tone was cutting. Belial stopped and slowly looked over his shoulder. The being who spoke wore a black tuxedo and had short, silver hair with a matching beard. His eyes were a bright, shimmering blue. But his stance was firm and confident. Belial noticed his hands were held in tight fists. His gaze was intense and his lips tense.

"Uriel," said Belial.

The crowd had parted and the idle conversation came to a halt. Belial and Uriel faced each other as everyone else gave them a wide berth. It was as if they were two gunslingers about to draw on each other.

"I asked you a question," said Uriel as he took a few steps closer. "What are you doing here, Belial?"

"I didn't come to start a fight, if that's what you think," said Belial. "I'm only here to talk."

"No one here is interested in anything a *demon* has to say."

"Five minutes, that's all I need."

"I wouldn't waste five minutes to piss on you," said Uriel.

"Not you," said Belial. "I came to speak with Anael."

Uriel scoffed. "You must be joking. I heard about the last time the two of you 'spoke.' In fact, the way it was told to me, seems you got your demonic ass handed to you."

Belial's eyes narrowed. "Watch yourself, angel. As I recall, you were never much of a fighter yourself. And I've eons of battle experience on you."

There was just the slightest hint of fear that flashed in Uriel's eyes. A tiny twitch of facial muscles. With those subtle signs, Belial knew that his intimidation tactics were working on the angel.

"You're boring me, Belial," said Uriel. "We both know even you aren't crazy enough to start a fight in Eden. With so many witnesses, no less. The Choir has been generous with your situation. But if you push your luck, they'll push back."

"This is the part where you tell me that's not a threat, but a promise."

"No, it actually *is* a threat," said Uriel. "This is me threatening you."

"If so, then it's fairly underwhelming," said Belial.

"Listen, you—"

Azure flames exploded in the space between the two celestials. At first, Belial assumed Uriel had made the first strike. But when he looked at the angel, he saw the same surprise etched on Uriel's face that Belial himself had felt.

"Zip up, boys. Nobody cares how big they are."

The new voice was also the source of the soulfire. Anael stood at the front of the crowd, her blue eyes pulsing and a small aura of flames surrounding the hand that hung casually at her side, the other hand resting on her hip.

Uriel approached Anael and spoke to her in a whisper. But it was still just barely loud enough for Belial to hear.

"I can handle this myself. I don't need your help," he said.

"It's fine, Uriel. I'll talk to him," she said.

"Are you serious? He violated the sanctity of Eden. If we give him what he wants, do you know what sort of message that will send?"

"I don't know nor do I care," said Anael.

"You'd better start caring—"

"Weak," said Belial.

Uriel turned back to the demon. "Excuse me?"

"That's the message people will receive if you do as I say," said Belial. "That you're weak."

"You heretical sack of shit…" muttered Uriel, taking a step closer to Belial.

In response, the demon simply folded his arms over his chest and smirked. "Raziel wouldn't take this shit from anyone—angel or demon. But you would never have been enough to fill his halo."

Uriel's eyes burned with anger and he raised his hand, soulfire starting to spark around his fingertips. Anael put her hand on his arm and gently but firmly pushed it back down to his side.

"Again, nobody cares," she said before turning to Belial. "You wanted five minutes. I'll grant you that audience, under the condition that you remain civil throughout."

Belial's smirk faded and his lips tightened in sincerity. He nodded. "You have my word."

"Good, then let's step outside."

Anael moved from Uriel and walked past Belial. He followed her, while every single eye in Eden remained locked on the pair. Uriel's anger at being upstaged still hung in the air like a pleasant aroma. They walked out onto the balcony and Anael went to the edge. She leaned over the railing and didn't even look at Belial as she spoke.

"I thought I made myself clear during our last meeting," she said. "I reached out to the Adversary in friendship, to help him put a stop to the necromancer. But his arrogance and paranoia wouldn't let him accept that. So tell me, why did he send you to come begging for my help?"

Belial wanted to respond in anger, but he knew that would get him nowhere. He had to keep his emotions in check and focus on what was truly important—getting his master the help he needed.

"He didn't send me," said Belial. "Quite the contrary, if he knew I were here, I doubt he'd be too pleased."

"You've got my attention, if nothing else."

"Barbatos. That's who the necromancer is," said Belial.

Anael looked back with a furrowed brow. "The beastmaster? Why would he be raising zombies?"

"I have no idea, but I suspect Lucifer might have uncovered the reason."

"'Suspect'? You mean he hasn't told you anything?"

asked Anael. "Is that why you came? You think he might trust *me* more than you?"

"No, that thought would never have even crossed my mind," said Belial. "We were separated for just a short period and in that time, Barbatos took the Morningstar captive. I had managed to find them, but not before…"

Belial hushed, feeling something in his throat that almost stopped him from talking. It wasn't something physically wrong with him, but it was connected to a form of emotion he wasn't familiar with. And Anael had apparently noticed it as well, because now she looked at him with concern.

"What is it?" she asked. "What's happened to him?"

CHAPTER 18

Out on the balcony of Eden, with a collection of celestials and well-connected humans watching from inside, Belial explained Lucifer's current state to Anael. He told her all about the attacks inflicted by Barbatos and how Lucifer currently lay near death. Belial came to Eden because he'd hoped Anael would put aside their differences and help the man she had once loved in eons past.

"I'm sorry," she said, "but I can't help you."

It was not the answer Belial had expected. Though he had no lost love for Anael—or any angel for that matter—he'd expected her to be merciful. In the past, she'd certainly proven amenable to granting Lucifer aid. So under these circumstances, he thought there was no way she'd refuse.

He was wrong.

"Perhaps you didn't hear me correctly," said Belial. "Lucifer. Is. *Dying*. If you don't use your powers to heal him, I doubt he'll survive much longer."

"And how did he come to this point?" asked Anael. "What was the first domino that knocked over the others?"

He knew what she meant, but he didn't want to give voice to it. Because in part, he could see where she was coming from.

"That's not the point," he said.

"The fact that you don't want to answer seems to suggest it is," said Anael. "There were options, Belial. You know this. The Adversary *chose* to abdicate the throne. He *chose* to refuse my help by throwing accusations in my face. And those choices led him to his fate."

"So you're going to let the Morningstar die because he hurt your feelings?"

"That's not it and fuck you for thinking I'd be that shallow," said Anael. "He doesn't like taking responsibility for his actions. That's always been his Achilles' heel. He has to face some consequences for the path he chose."

"Then let me ask you something, Miss Perfect: how is he supposed to learn from his mistakes if he's dead?"

Anael didn't respond with words, but she instead turned away. "I'm sorry. But I can't be there to bail him out whenever he screws up his life."

"Fine." Belial turned away from her and started to move back towards the elevator. "Then when the Infernal Court asks what happened, I'll let them know the forces of Heaven had the opportunity to spare Lucifer and instead stood by as he lay dying. Then you can explain to your masters why war is on the horizon."

He had almost reached the balcony doors when Anael called out to him again. Belial stopped but wouldn't look back at her. He just waited to hear what else she had to say, though he doubted it would prove to be anything of significance.

"Just because I won't help him doesn't mean he has to die," said Anael. "I'm sure you have other avenues that you haven't even considered pursuing yet. Maybe in all that time of working by Lucifer's side, you've learned a little something about the importance of striking bargains, haven't you?"

Belial didn't respond, but walked back into Eden. He moved past the onlookers with a quick stride and didn't even acknowledge Uriel as he walked by him. The demon went straight for the elevator and left the world of the angels behind.

Another option, one he hadn't even considered? Who else could possibly be capable of healing Lucifer? Surely she didn't mean taking him to Hell? Just seeing the Morningstar in such a state would rile up the demons. Some legitimately would be angered and others would use it as an opportunity. And Belial didn't trust Cross enough to know if he could be relied upon in this situation. Certainly there wasn't anyone in Purgatory who could provide help.

The elevator reached the ground floor and Belial exited. He kept running through every possibility in his mind and it wasn't until he reached a secluded alleyway that the idea came to him.

No, they'd never agree to it, he though to himself. But the other thing Anael said hit him—a bargain. That just might give him the leverage he needed to convince them. It was certainly a long shot, but it wasn't as if Belial had an abundance of options.

His wings emerged and wrapped around him, teleporting him away from Chicago.

"Dammit!"

Samara kicked her folded leg out, hitting the cloth on which her bone set lay. The cloth folded over and the bones scattered across the motel room floor. She sighed and straightened out the cloth, then collected the bones and placed them back in the center.

Isaiah had gone to speak to the sheriff about the latest attacks. Some kids had been accosted by a zombie just last night—two dead, one injured. She told him to go on alone while she stayed behind to try and get a read on whatever was causing this.

Her grandmother had trained her in hoodoo since she was young. Samara had mostly gone along with the teachings, never expecting them to amount to much. Little did she know that years later, she'd end up using those talents as a member of Uncle Sam's only paranormal intelligence agency.

Unfortunately, they weren't helping her at the moment. The spirits weren't talking much, which could mean that they were frightened of whoever this necromancer was. Or something was keeping them quiet.

Isaiah's investigation wasn't liable to turn up anything useful, which meant it was all on her and her little bones to get the job done. Only problem was she wasn't sure she could actually accomplish anything.

Just as she prepared another attempt at throwing the bones, Samara was blinded by a yellow light. The bones fell out of her hands and she raised one of her arms to shield her eyes from the brightness. It faded almost as quickly as it came, revealing a tall, broad-shouldered man with a bald head and bat-like wings.

Samara jumped from the floor and quickly stepped back until she found the table in the corner of the room. She drew her weapon from the holster and aimed it right at the intruder's head.

"I'm pretty sure you recognize the markings on the barrel," she said, gesturing to the sigils engraved into the metal.

Belial held his hands up as his wings receded into his back. "I thought we had an understanding, Agent Tillman."

"Note the past tense," said Samara. "Or did you forget about how you scurried out of here as soon as you got what you needed?"

"The Morningstar was in grave danger, I didn't have any time to hesitate. I did what I had to do," said Belial. "If it were your partner who was in danger, would you have done any less?"

Samara took a slow breath and gradually lowered her gun. "No, I suppose not." She didn't set down the weapon, just held it at her side, with her index finger resting just outside the trigger guard. "So why *did* you come back?"

"Because I still need your help." Belial glanced down at the bones lying on the cloth. "And judging from the looks of things, you could use some as well."

"What if you're wrong?" she asked. "What if we're doing just fine without you?"

"One look at your face tells me that you're not exactly being truthful."

Samara sighed. Having a chat with a demon instead of just shooting him in the face and getting it over with. She must have taken complete leave of her senses. Yet, Belial was right. Their investigation had gone nowhere.

"Say we could use some help. There's always a catch, isn't there?" she asked.

"Those bones and the power I sensed within you," said Belial. "You're a witch, aren't you?"

"I prefer practitioner," said Samara.

"Whatever you call yourself, you *do* possess the ability to work spells, yes?"

"You know I do."

"Have you ever done a healing spell?"

Samara cocked an eyebrow. "Yes…but why would a demon need one? Those only work on mortals."

"That's why I need one. There's…" Belial paused, "…a…mortal. One who needs healing."

"Who?"

"Are you still interested in honoring our deal?" asked Belial. "You help me with my problem, I help you close your case."

"If I were to agree to anything—and I'm not saying I am—I'd still need to know more first."

"What I'm proposing is—"

BANG!

A gunshot echoed in the room. As soon as the shot was fired, Belial turned. He was struck instantly in the shoulder. The force of the blow staggered him and he dropped to one knee.

Samara brought her weapon up in a reflexive response and aimed in the direction the shot came from. Belial himself recovered fairly quickly, his teeth gritted to fight through the pain. His eyes burned bright and hellfire ignited within the palm of his hand.

"Oh shit," she muttered and lowered her gun.

Isaiah stepped in through the door linking the two rooms. His arms were raised and the still-smoking barrel of his gun aimed right at Belial's face. Like Samara, it seemed he wasn't happy about how Belial had just run out on them before.

"Shouldn't have come back, Hellspawn," he said.

"Actually, I used to be an angel," said Belial. "So technically, I'm Heavenspawn."

"Don't give a good goddamn *where* you came from," said Isaiah. "All I know is I'm about to send you back there."

"Zay, calm down," said Samara.

"Not a chance, partner," said Isaiah. "We gave this demon a shot once already and he welched. So the next shot I give him is going to be right between his bright little eyes."

"I did what I had to do to save my master," said Belial. "The Morningstar was in danger. And in fact, he still is."

"He's willing to help us if we help him," said Samara.

"That's what he said just a few hours ago. Then he up and vanished," said Isaiah. "Why should we trust him again?"

"Because you have no other options," said Belial. "Barbatos is too dangerous for two mortals to take on alone. And you'll never even find him unless you know what Lucifer has already learned about his plans."

"What did he find out?" asked Samara.

"The only person who knows is Lucifer," said Belial. "And if you want that information, you'll need to help me."

"Not buying it," said Isaiah.

"And what exactly have you learned on your own, Agent Reeves?" asked Belial. "Please, enlighten me."

Isaiah hesitated. His eyes wavered, fluttering briefly to the side before returning to Belial. And he scoffed. "Like I'd tell you."

He was covering and Samara knew it. She had worked with Isaiah long enough to know when he was being honest and when he was lying through his teeth.

"We don't know anything, you're right about that," she said.

"Samara!" Isaiah barked.

"Sorry, Zay, but it's the truth," said Samara, then turned to Belial. "But it seems you don't know much either. So if we're going to work together on this, then there are still some things *I* need to know. Like who exactly do you need a healing spell for?"

Belial sighed and closed his hand, extinguishing the hellfire. He sat on the bed, cringing at his wounded shoulder. "It's for Lucifer."

"Now you want us to help you keep the Devil alive?" asked Isaiah. "Samara, do you *not* hear how crazy this sounds?"

"Maybe it's crazy, but we just keep hitting walls doing this on our own," said Samara. "And how many more people will die while we keep chasing our tails? It won't cost us a thing to hear him out."

Isaiah's nostrils flared. He obviously wasn't happy about it, but Samara knew he trusted her. And in the end, that's why he finally relented and lowered his weapon.

"Thank you," said Belial. "To answer your question, Lucifer was attacked by Barbatos. And in his mortal state, he was left near-death. I cannot work a healing spell on my own. My powers don't work that way. Mostly I'm just built to destroy things, not restore them. So if I'm to learn what Lucifer knows, then first I need to find a way to heal him. If you're willing to come with me, to heal his wounds, then I'm certain he'd return the favor by providing you with what you need."

"So, Samara works her mojo on Satan, we stop Barbatos, and then what?" asked Isaiah. "What happens to the demon once the dust settles?"

"In your line of work, I assume lethal force is authorized," said Belial.

"It's how we take out most threats, yes," said Samara.

"That's what we want, too," said Belial. "If Barbatos is killed, then all four of us go home content."

Samara locked eyes with Isaiah and then she said, "Belial, could you step outside and give us some privacy? I'd like to talk it over with my partner.

Belial nodded. "Of course. I'll be right outside." He opened the front door and stepped out into the parking lot.

"It's insane," said Isaiah.

"You were willing to give him a chance before."

"That was before he disappeared and before he asked you to heal Satan."

"Do I think it's ideal? Hell no," said Samara. "But we've got nothing else. The longer this goes on, the more bodies that are going to pile up. We've got to find out what's happening here and helping that demon is the only path I see to getting some answers."

Isaiah shook his head. "You don't know that."

"I don't?" she asked. "Okay then. Tell me what other options we have. Tell me one piece of evidence our investigation has turned up. What exactly have we accomplished here?"

Isaiah opened his mouth, sighed, and then closed it again. He fidgeted in place, but whenever it seemed like he was going to say something, he remained silent.

"You've got a point," he said. "But I still don't think this is a good idea."

"I never said it was a good idea," said Samara. "Just that it's the only one we've got."

CHAPTER 19

Samara walked slowly through the bedroom door Belial had opened for her. The master bedroom was larger than some studio apartments she'd seen. And pushed up against the wall was a massive, four-poster king-size bed. Just being in here felt crazy to her—she was about to save the Devil's life.

Belial and Isaiah remained by the door, just watching from a distance. Isaiah had his arms folded and a terse look on his face. But in the demon's eyes she saw only concern. It was a strange look on him, to see him so…human.

She felt a similar sensation when she approached the side of the bed and saw Lucifer lying there. Completely oblivious to the world, with the sheets and comforter pulled up to his neck. She was gentle as she pulled them back to reveal his body—naked save for the dressings Belial had applied to the wounds. Samara knelt down by the side of the bed and placed her bag on the floor beside her. She reached out to his neck and felt for his carotid artery. He had a pulse but it was certainly weak.

"Can you do it?" asked Belial.

Samara hesitated before answering the demon's question. *Could* she? *Should* she? This was her idea, she knew that, but she'd been second-guessing herself ever since she'd first agreed to it.

"Agent Tillman?" the demon asked again.

"I don't know!" she finally answered with audible exasperation. She repeated the words, this time in almost a whisper: "I don't know…"

"We had a deal. You said—"

"The deal was I would *try*," she said. "The healing spell, it's for humans after all. Even if he's lost his powers, Lucifer still isn't really a human. He's not even really an angel or a demon. He's…" She looked at his soft, handsome features, "…unique."

"Do whatever you would do for a human, then," said Belial. "There are no other options. No one else I can go to."

She didn't say another word, just opened the bag and reached inside to draw out a small pair of scissors. Samara stood and leaned over Lucifer's body, bringing the scissors over to his dark hair. She clipped the edges off a few strands and they fell into her waiting palm.

"What are you doing?" asked Belial.

"Take it easy," said Isaiah, moving in front of the demon. "My girl knows what she's doing."

I hope you're right about that, Zay, she thought to herself. "The spell requires a doll made in the likeness of the person. That means I need something from him, like hair or fingernail clippings."

She reached into the bag again and took out a small, featureless doll made of white fabric. With the scissors, she made a slit in the doll's body and inserted the hair inside. Samara took a small kit with needles already threaded. She selected one and quickly stitched the cut she'd made in the doll, then set it next to Lucifer.

"This isn't like any spell I've seen before," said Belial.

"Magic is about focusing your energies. The rituals are just a tool to do so," said Samara. "That's why they vary from culture to culture."

She took out a white candle and two vials of oils. One was a healing oil, the other sage. After pouring a few dabs of each oil into her palm, she rubbed the candle in them. Once placing the candle on the ground in front of her, Samara lit the wick. She then drew out a few containers of herbs—bay leaves, sage, eucalyptus, rosemary, and sprinkled them in few separate piles.

Samara took the doll and whispered a prayer to call on the power of Loko. He was one of the loa, the spirits practitioners served in order to work their wills. Loko was the patron of healers and plants and considered the first houngan.

Once she finished the prayer, she blew gently on the doll, then took a bit of the crushed bay leaves and cast them into the candle's flame. The herbs sizzled and burned as they hit the fire. She whispered the incantation again and this time, tossed the sage into the flame. Samara repeated this process with each of the herbs in order.

When the last of the herbs had been burned, Samara placed the doll on Lucifer's chest. She then picked up the candle and stood over him, holding it in both hands. Samara raised the candle up to her head, then brought it down to her waist, and finally from her left shoulder to her right. Then, she blew the flame out and set the candle down on the beside.

"Is that it?" asked Belial.

"For now," she said.

Belial came up beside her and looked down at Lucifer's prone form. "Nothing's changed. Why has nothing changed? You did the spell, didn't you?"

"It's not instantaneous," said Samara. "For now, it's out of our hands. We just have to wait and see if the spell takes."

"Wait for how long?" asked Belial.

Samara shrugged. "Depends on the person and the severity of injuries. I can't promise it even *will* work."

"But—"

She placed a hand on his shoulder. She could sense the hurt in his voice, and she wasn't sure how one went about comforting a demon. But she wanted to try anyway.

"Belial, please. Just be patient and have faith."

He looked at her and scoffed. "If you knew him, you would understand how ludicrous he'd find that statement."

"Yeah, well, my power's based on faith. So I need you to just go with it, okay?"

Belial gave a nod.

"Come on," she said. "Let's give him some space and time to heal."

Lucifer's eyes slowly flickered open. His mouth was dry and his entire body felt lethargic. When he pulled himself up to a sitting position and leaned his back against the bed's headboard, he was surprised to see the small, white doll roll down his chest and fall into his lap. Curiously, he raised it to his eye level and turned it over several times, trying to figure out where it came from and what purpose it served.

He dropped it on the bedside table and that's when he noticed the candle with the burnt wick. Lucifer swung his legs over the edge of the mattress and picked up the candle next, also examining it. He brought the fingers that touched the wax up to his nose and sniffed them. Then he took a whiff of the wick.

Herbal scents still lingered on both. Sage…eucalyptus…rosemary…

Replacing the candle, Lucifer looked down at his own body. There were so many bandages held to his skin by surgical tape that he felt he'd been mummified. What was the last thing that had happened?

Lucifer closed his eyes and reached through the fog of his memory. In an instant, it all came flooding back to him—Barbatos whisking him away to an animal sanctuary, then Lucifer having to try to fight off several vicious tigers. After that…

No, that was it. That was where the memory had stopped. He was nearly killed—he *should* have been killed. There seemed no reason for Barbatos to let him go free and Lucifer knew he didn't have the strength to survive on his own.

Yet here he was, lying in his own bed. Lucifer figured it must have been Belial who came to his rescue. Though *how* he was able to find Lucifer in the first place was still a question. Seemed obvious from the doll and the candle that Belial had asked someone for help to speed up the healing process.

Lucifer pulled the sheets from his legs and saw he was naked. First thing he wanted to do was take a shower before answering any of those questions.

He climbed out of bed and walked towards the master bathroom. His movements were sluggish and his joints stiff. How long had it been since the tiger attack?

LUCIFER BOUND

Inside the bathroom, Lucifer turned on the light and lookd at himself in the mirror. He reached down and started picking at the edges of the tape, then pulled on it to peel the strips off. The bandages came loose and fell. One after the other, until they all ended up in a bloodstained pile on the bathroom floor.

Lucifer moved closer to the mirror and started to move his fingers over the wounds. They'd all closed up, leaving pink scars in their place. Claw and tooth marks all over his torso, his arms, legs—even his neck. With each piece of scar tissue he touched, a memory flashed of the wound inflicted by one of the tigers. They all came at him in vivid recall, and Lucifer nearly stumbled and fell over from the onslaught.

He regained his bearings and shook his head to clear the memories. Lucifer kicked away the pile of gauze and tape and opened the glass door to step into the shower.

The hot water felt envigorating as it washed over his body. He switched the shower head to powerful jets and allowed them the massage the fatigue from his weary muscles. Lucifer stood there under the water with his eyes closed, tensing and flexing every muscle the water hit to get them back into something that felt like normalcy.

After washing his body with soap and a good rinse, Lucifer turned off the water. He opened the door and reached for a towel hanging on the rack and worked slowly to dry himself off.

He left the towel on the bathroom floor and then walked back into the master bedroom. Lucifer dressed quickly and simply in a pair of black jeans and a black t-shirt, then left the room and went down the ornate wooden staircase.

"Belial!" he shouted into the house as he reached the

first floor and turned the corner. "Belial, we need to talk about what I miss—"

Once stepping inside the kitchen, Lucifer was stunned to see the two OSIRIS agents in his house. Samara Tillman was sitting at the kitchen table with Belial while Isaiah Reeves stood in front of the stove.

"And apparently, I missed quite a lot," said Lucifer.

Surprise was worn on the three faces that looked back at the Morningstar. Belial got over it the quickest and stood. He moved in front of Lucifer and knelt down on one knee.

"I apologize, my lord," he said in a soft tone. "I failed in my duty as your protector. I should have been there when Barbatos—"

Lucifer rolled his eyes at the supplication. "Stand up, man. You're embarrassing me in front of the shadowy government agents."

Belial rose up. "I apologize for my candor."

"Instead of bowing and scraping, you could tell me about our new guests." Lucifer took an empty seat at the table. "Agents Tillman and Reeves, if I remember correctly."

"You remembered correctly," said Isaiah, turning his attention back to the stove. With his back to the others, Lucifer couldn't see what exactly the agent was cooking. But it smelled good enough.

"Belial found us at the motel, used my power to try and locate you," said Samara.

"I found where Barbatos had taken you. I dispatched the beasts and then brought you back here," said Belial, now having returned to his own seat. "But I needed aid in healing you. Agent Tillman was the only one I could turn to."

"The only one?" asked Lucifer. "What about Mara?"

"She temporarily returned to Hell and her underlings at Lust didn't know when she'd return."

"No one else?" asked Lucifer. "Not even…" His voice grew softer before he spoke the name. And judging from the look on his face, Belial knew exactly who he was referring to.

"She refused," he said.

Lucifer felt like the wind had been knocked out of his chest. "Did she give a reason?"

"She said you had to live with the consequences of the choices you made."

Lucifer sighed. "Sounds like her…" he muttered with a hint of melancholy. He didn't want to succumb to feelings of despair, so he chose to focus on what was more important. "So, you went to Agent Tillman for help after that."

"Yeah, we came to an agreement," said Samara. "If I healed you, then we get your help on taking down Barbatos."

Lucifer turned his gaze onto Belial again and began to smirk. "*You* made a deal?"

Belial just looked down.

"Well, who says you can't teach an old demon new tricks?" Lucifer then turned back to Samara. "So, your spell…hoodoo?"

"Yeah," she said.

"I thought so." Lucifer pulled up his shirt to show off the abs beneath that were marred with pink scars. He patted them. "Very good work."

"Thanks…" said Samara, evidently trying not to stare at his muscles.

Lucifer smiled to himself and put his shirt back in place. "How long has it been?"

"Since the attack?" asked Belial. "About a week."

"And you've all just been sitting here in that time?" asked Lucifer.

"Hardly." Isaiah joined the conversation, carrying two plates. He set one in fromt of Samara and one in front of Lucifer. A quick return to the counter and he brought back two more plates—one for himself and Belial.

Lucifer examined the sandwich and bit into it. Bread greased with burnt butter and melted cheese filled his mouth. There were also some spices that went along with it.

"Samara and I have mostly been spending our time back in Louisiana, trying to figure this out," said Isaiah. "We've been trying to dig up some clues, but so far, nothing much."

"Okay," said Lucifer once he swallowed the mouthful of grilled cheese. "Tell me everything you know."

CHAPTER 20

After they finished eating lunch, Lucifer invited them into the library where he fit into his favorite high-backed chair like a glove. Both Samara and Isaiah chose to take the couch and Belial just stood beside Lucifer's chair with his arms folded.

Even without the guilt Belial had expressed earlier, Lucifer would still be able to have sensed the demon's remorse. It came off him in waves that didn't require any sort of empathic ability to pick up on.

"So far, the zombie attacks have mostly been concentrated in Metairie. Seems that's where Barbatos is concentrating his efforts for the time being. Thing I can't seem to understand is why," said Isaiah.

"From what he told me, it was more or less happenstance that he began in Metairie, but his goals are far loftier," said Lucifer. "Agent Reeves is right, seems strange for Barbatos to remain confined to a small New Orleans suburb."

"What exactly did Barbatos say he wanted to do?" asked Samara.

"Essentially start the zombie apocalypse," said Lucifer. "Barbatos wishes to raise all the corpses and turn them on the living."

"And let me guess, he's doing it just for the fun," said Samara.

"As a matter of fact, no," said Lucifer. "Demons are just as complex as you humans. They have different motivations for their actions. Some are just interested in destruction for the sake of it, but there are certainly examples of that mentality within mankind as well."

"Wish I could argue that point with you, but I've seen enough to know otherwise," said Isaiah.

"Precisely. But then there are others who do things for a reason," said Lucifer. "Barbatos was something of a beastmaster before The Fall. He watched over the animals of the world. And their treatment by humans angered him, so he attempted to spur them to rise up against the beings he perceived as their oppressors."

"This isn't the Planet of the Apes, so obviously he didn't succeed," said Samara. "So what happened?"

"I did," said Belial.

Samara gave the demon a curious look, but Belial said nothing further.

"You can think of Belial as sort of my own personal bounty hunter," said Lucifer. "Whenever I learned that one of Hell's denizens threatened the armistice with Heaven, I dispatched him to drag them back and imprison them in Cocytus. Barbatos was one such instance. But now, he's trying a different tactic. Instead of turning animals against the humans, he's having humans literally consume themselves. Because in his mind, that's exactly what you'd eventually do to this world. He wants to see you do it to yourselves and spare the planet."

"What are you so worried about?" asked Samara. "Just

turn the big guy on him again. If he took Barbatos down once—"

"I'm afraid it's not that simple," said Lucifer.

Samara deflated. "Never is, is it?"

"Barbatos seems to have grown stronger than he was before. He wasn't even a necromancer in the past but somehow, he managed to master that skill in a very short amount of time," said Lucifer. "And now, we could be looking at a situation where he might very well have the power to do what he plans."

Samara shook her head. "No, you're wrong."

Lucifer's head snapped in her direction. "I'm sorry, could you say that again?"

"What you're saying, it's not possible," said Samara. "No necromancer would have the kind of power you'd need to raise *that* many corpses."

"What about that thing at the cemetery?" asked Isaiah.

Samara glanced at her partner. "That was dozens. You're talking potentially billions of zombies. It's just not possible. He'd die from exhaustion before he even got a fraction of the way there. And remember, these zombies aren't like the ones in the movies. If they bite you, you'd be at risk of getting a nasty infection, but you won't become a zombie yourself."

"So no way for them to reproduce and no way for him to raise the army he'd need. Once you take out the corpses, the problem's solved," said Isaiah. "As far as doomsday plans are concerned, seems like a pretty poor one once you break it down."

Lucifer rubbed his chin while he thought back to his confrontation with the demon. And he remembered that he and Barbatos had spoken of the power it would take to do such a thing.

"Barbatos had something else in mind. He planned on some way to get the power he needed in order to enact his plan," said Lucifer.

"What's that?" asked Isaiah.

"I don't know, he wouldn't tell me," said Lucifer. "But he seemed pretty sure of himself."

"Could it involve Death?" asked Belial.

Isaiah sat up straight and raised a hand. "Hold up…did you just say Death? As in *the* Death?"

"Yes," said Lucifer.

"Grim Reaper, got a thing for cloaks and scythes, likes to ride around on a pale horse?" asked Isaiah. "*That* Death, right?"

"He's a little…different from the popular conception, but yes, we are talking about the personification of Death," said Lucifer. "However, to answer Belial's question, no. I don't believe Death is involved in any way, shape, or form."

"Why not?" asked Samara.

"For one thing, Death doesn't think much of us. He's been around long before this planet and long before Heaven for that matter. He'd have as much interest in the plans of a rogue demon as you'd have in the plans of a subatomic particle," said Lucifer.

"I…*think* that's a relief…?" said Samara.

"Trust me, it is," said Lucifer. "But beyond that fact, this kind of thing wouldn't really be Death's purview. Getting a soul to go back into a corpse, that would be something he'd do. But Barbatos doesn't need these zombies to possess souls—in fact, that would be contrary to his goals."

Isaiah huffed and stood from the couch. He walked

over to the fireplace and rested his arm on the mantle, staring into the blackened stone. Finally, he looked at Lucifer.

"Aren't you gonna do something?" he asked.

"What do you think I'm trying to do?" asked Lucifer.

"We're not the experts here," said Isaiah, gesturing to himself.

"Actually, we kind of are," said Samara.

Isaiah tossed his partner an angry look. "You *know* what I meant. Compared to him—" now he gestured at Lucifer, "—we're goddamn amateurs."

"At least we agree on something," said Belial.

Isaiah pointed at the demon. "We had a deal, big guy. We fix up your master and you help us take down Barbatos. Now we've lived up to our side, so when are you going to live up to yours?"

"What would you like me to do, Agent Reeves?" asked Lucifer. "I can't tell you something I don't know. If there is some source of power or spell Barbatos is after, I haven't the first clue what it could be."

"You're the Devil, aren't you supposed to know all this stuff?"

"I'm a fallen angel, that doesn't make me omniscient. There is much about this world that even us celestials don't understand. We're other-dimensional beings, not gods."

Samara's back straightened as a thought came to her. "But you're not the only ones, right?"

"What are you talking about?" asked Isaiah.

"Angels and demons, you're not the only celestials or whatever out there, are you?" she asked. "There are other things. Things not connected to you guys."

"Yes, that's true," said Lucifer. "Faeries, for example. Demigods as well. Why?"

"The loa."

"The *what*?" asked Isaiah.

"They're the spirits voodoo and hoodoo practitioners call upon when we're using our spells. That's where our power comes from," said Samara. "Different loa have different purposes, much like the gods and goddesses of mythology."

"I confess to not knowing much about the beings outside of the realm of Heaven and Hell," said Lucifer. "Do you really think there are any loa who are capable of granting Barbatos that kind of power?"

"Capable, yes," said Samara. "But *would* they do it? That's a different story. We don't command the loa, we only appeal to them."

"But *could* they?" asked Lucifer. "Are the loa capable of being manipulated or even enslaved?"

"I don't think there's any being in the universe that's immune to either," said Samara. "But you're the expert on celestials, so you tell me—could it happen to any of your kind?"

Could an angel be manipulated and enslaved? That was essentially what the Divine Choir had done to all of them. Eons of slavery and they still didn't even realize it. Forced into a life of servitude while bound by invisible chains. Some might even say many of the demons in Hell were in a similar boat. They worshipped the Morningstar as their god, despite his repeated attempts to get them to stop. Even Belial, who knew him personally and lived with him, had trouble getting past that sort of devotion.

"My answer would be an unequivocal yes," said Lucifer. "Barbatos seemed incredibly sure of himself, though. Is there a loa who deals with death?"

"Oh yeah." There was a knowing tone in her reply, suggesting that she knew—but possibly feared—where this discussion would eventually end up. "The Guédé. They're the loa family of death and fertility. And their leader is considered the master of the dead, who is responsible for keeping corpses in the ground."

"Seems he's been sleeping on the job, then," said Isaiah.

"In our traditions, necromancy is accomplished by making offerings and requests of him. He's also willing to make deals, but only if he likes the offering," said Samara. "He has many names, but we know him as Baron Samedi."

The name rung in Lucifer's mind. Throughout his time in Hell, he kept to himself, but observed the worlds around. He'd heard mention of Baron Samedi in the past, but it always seemed to be the stuff of legends. Was it possible, he wondered, for these loa to have some connection to Purgatory and Thanatos, the embodiment of that realm? Or were the Guédé servants of Death himself?

Those were intriguing questions, but also best left for another time. What Lucifer needed to concentrate on now was finding out exactly how Barbatos planned to appeal to Samedi.

"It's all about striking deals then, isn't it?" asked Lucifer. "Samedi would only act if the terms were favorable to him."

"Unless Barbatos has found some way to capture the Baron," said Samara.

"There is always a way," said Belial. "I do not know what specifically Barbatos will do, but if he's so certain of his victory, then he must have a contingency plan should Samedi refuse the deal. Perhaps an artifact or an arcane ritual."

"Or he won't even plan to deal in the first place," said

Lucifer. "Presumably, Samedi would know if there's something out there capable of controlling him, right?"

Samara gave a little shrug. "Sure, I suppose. But what's that got to do with anything?"

"We arrange a meeting," said Lucifer.

Isaiah scoffed. "That's a stupid idea."

The demon's muscles tensed and his hands curled into tight fists. "Watch your tongue!"

Lucifer held up his hand to defuse his protector. "It's all right, Belial. If Agent Reeves has a critique, I want to hear it."

Isaiah moved from the fireplace behind the couch. He rested his forearms on the back and leaned forward. "Think about it this way. Imagine you're Superman and you were the only one who knew about kryptonite. Would you go to Lois Lane and tell her to write a story about it, or would you keep it locked up in your arctic fortress?"

"I see your point. Maybe not the way I would have articulated it, but the example is clear enough," said Lucifer.

"Assuming there is something out there that can control this guy, I really doubt he'll squawk about it to anyone, let alone the Devil," said Isaiah. "I know I wouldn't."

"You make a good point, but I believe it's worth any potential risk." Lucifer looked at Samara. "Is it possible? Could you do it?"

Samara sighed. "I've made appeals to the loa before, but never one of the Guédé family. And certainly not Baron Samedi himself. I've also never arranged an actual face-to-face meeting with any loa before. This is uncharted territory for me." She looked at Isaiah. "Do I call this in? We're talking something bigger than the usual spells I work with."

"Are you saying you need permission?" asked Lucifer.

"We're federal agents," said Isaiah. "That means we have to get authorization when we break out the big guns."

"I don't know if they'd approve something like this," said Samara. "Especially considering the circumstances…"

"Doesn't matter, we've gotta try." Isaiah stood upright and took his phone from his pocket. "I'll make the call."

Lucifer watched carefully as Isaiah left the room to put in the request to his superiors at OSIRIS. But the Morningstar knew the chances of them approving such a request were pretty much nonexistent. His eyes drifted back to Samara.

He needed to meet with Baron Samedi. And for that, he needed Samara Tillman to perform the necessary ritual. That meant Isaiah Reeves now stood in the way of his mission…

CHAPTER 21

saiah walked out to the patio deck overlooking the in-
ground pool. He had his phone in hand and dialed the
number, holding it to his ear as he waited for the other
side. A moment later came an automated request asking
to enter his authentication code. Isaiah quickly tapped in
a series of numbers with his thumb. A few more moments
passed until finally, a gruff voice answered on the other end.

"Sir, it's Reeves," said Isaiah.

"Reeves? How come the ping shows you're in Illinois?
That's not exactly Louisiana, which is where I sent you and
Tillman."

"I know, sir. The investigation has led us into some…
interesting areas. And that's actually why I'm calling."

"What sort of areas?"

"We think we've got a game plan to take out the guy
responsible for this. Problem is, we're going to have to
summon up some pretty big-league magic to do so."

There was a groan on the other end, followed by the
clacking of fingers on a keyboard. Then finally, his superior
spoke again. "What sort of spell are we talking about here?"

"Sir, I assume you know what the loa are?"

"Reeves, I've been at this job since you were knee-high

to a grasshopper. Of fucking course I know what the loa are. You calling me incompetent?"

"Sorry, sir. Of course not, sir," said Isaiah. "The point is in order to proceed with our plan, we need authorization to arrange for a meeting with one of the loa."

"Which one?"

Isaiah hesitated. This was it, the moment of truth. He maintained some slim hope that maybe the question of which loa wouldn't come up. But now here it was and Isaiah had no choice but to answer.

"Baron Samedi."

The angry expletives that came from his superior's mouth were so loud, Isaiah had to hold the phone at arm's length. Even still, he could hear them pouring through the device. When the volume subsided just slightly, Isaiah pressed the phone back to his ear.

"Sir, I understand this is an unusual situation, but—"

"No, you listen to *me*, Reeves. Samedi is unpredictable as all get out and there's no guarantee you could control the situation if he decides to get off the reservation. This is fire you're playing with and I won't tolerate it. OSIRIS has enough problems to deal with. We don't need some voodoo death spirit or whatever running loose and causing chaos!"

"Yes, sir. I know it's a risky move. But we—"

"Besides, Tillman isn't qualified for that level of magic. She's cleared for simple spells and communing, not summoning up the loa for tea and crumpets."

"Yes, but sir—"

"But nothing. I'm not granting your authorization."

"Okay, then can I ask a question?" asked Isaiah, trying to contain his own rage as it bubbled up beneath the surface. "How the hell do you expect us to stop a demon who plans to take control of Samedi and start the zombie apocalypse?"

"No demon would be able to do such a thing, so you're starting from a false premise. Now you get your ass back to Metairie and you kill that sumbitch. If you can't do the job, then I'll find an agent who's willing to actually do what I fucking say!"

The call ended with that. Isaiah sighed and dropped the phone in his pocket. He turned away from the deck railing and experience a start when he saw Lucifer leaning against the back door, hands comfortable resting in his pockets.

"I suppose you heard that," said Isaiah.

"Enough of it," said Lucifer. "Seems your bosses aren't interested in helping us out."

"No shit. You should be a detective." Isaiah reached inside his jacket and took out a silver container. He opened it up to reveal a line of cigarillos. Isaiah took one for himself and offered the case to Lucifer.

"Thanks, but I'll pass," said Lucifer, holding up his hand.

"Suit yourself." Isaiah closed the container and put it back in his jacket pocket, then drew out a Zippo. He turned the flint wheel and once the flame sprung to life, held the edge of the cigarillo over the fire, puffing until he was sure it was properly lit.

"Does he know about me?"

The involuntary laugh the comment brought to Isaiah caused him to also let out a series of coughs. "Are you crazy? Of course he doesn't."

"Perhaps if you explained the situation in more detail…"

Isaiah held his thumb and forefinger up by the side

of his head. "'Sir, Agent Reeves again. I'm sorry, but I forgot to mention before that Satan's riding shotgun on this and he personally guarantees that summoning up the unpredictable, chaotic death guardian of the loa is actually a swell idea. What's the Devil even doing up here? Well, turns out he actually escaped from Hell and is responsible for this demon running loose in the first place.'" Isaiah's phone gesture turned into an open hand that he waved in an incredulous manner. "Are you fucking stoned?"

"Unfortunately not, but there's an idea," said Lucifer.

"I tell my boss about you, I'm liable to be locked up, too. We'd both be fucked six ways from Sunday."

Lucifer moved from the door to the spot beside Isaiah. He sat on the edge of the railing and issued a sigh. "Agent Reeves, what do you think of me?"

Reeves took the cigarillo from his mouth, a cloud of smoke floating over his face. The question was a strange one and he wasn't sure how he should answer. What did he think of the Devil? The answer should have been obvious, and yet…

"I honestly don't know what to make of you," he finally said. "You seem like you're on the level, but there's this…I can't explain it. Almost like a gut reaction whenever I look at you. Almost like a revulsion."

"Are you a religious man?"

"Not for a long time," said Isaiah.

"But you used to be?"

Isaiah hesitated and then gave a quick nod. "Yeah, was raised in a Baptist home. Pops was a preacher, actually."

"So what changed for you?" asked Lucifer.

Isaiah turned around and leaned over the railing while he puffed on the cigarillo. "When you watch a kid turn himself into a human bomb because your government lied about the reasons why hundreds of thousands of brown people deserved to die, you start to question a lot of things. Especially the fairy tale that there's some sort of higher power or reason to all this madness."

"Am I wrong in assuming you first learned of the supernatural when you joined OSIRIS?"

"No, you're right on the money," said Isaiah.

"And how did that make you feel? Baptist-turned-atheist being hit right in the face with confirmation of Heaven and Hell?"

"Hard to say," said Isaiah. "Demons, angels, magic—it all exists, that much I know. But questions about God are beyond my pay grade."

"Do you know the problem with most organized religions?" asked Lucifer.

"Their tax-exempt status?"

Lucifer chuckled. "Besides that."

"You got me."

"Doesn't matter what religion, doesn't matter which deity—monotheistic, polytheistic, whatever. All of them try to make sense of the world in a way that even the simplest person can understand."

"That's a bad thing?"

"You were a soldier, right?"

Isaiah took another puff on the cigarillo before he answered. "Yeah. Iraq."

"Who were the good guys in that war and who were the bad?"

Isaiah stood up. "That's not…there wasn't really—"

"What about Vietnam?"

"I think I get your point," said Isaiah. "You're saying

simplification isn't always a good thing."

"When I rebelled against Heaven, it wasn't because I'm some mustache-twirling supervillain," said Lucifer. "It wasn't good versus evil, it was differing ideologies, and those can have various levels of complexity. But like with any war, the winners get to write the history."

"That's all fascinating, though I don't get what any of this has to do with our current situation," said Isaiah.

"I'm not a bad guy is what I've been trying to tell you," said Lucifer. "I'm just a man."

"Actually…"

"You know what I mean," said Lucifer. "I'm not interested in conquering the world or corrupting souls or whatever sort of nonsense organized religion and pop culture have filled your head with. What I really want is to put a stop to this demon that's running loose."

"A demon you're responsible for."

Lucifer huffed. "Yes, I'm aware of my role in this. But if you stick to following orders, then we won't be able to stop Barbatos. And then, you will share equally in the responsibility of what happens to mankind."

Isaiah looked down, taking a few more puffs. He stared at the polished black shoes, reflecting the afternoon sunlight off their surface. "If we do this and we're found out, it could end up very bad for us. Even associating with you, if it's uncovered, will be impossible to explain."

"What's the worst that will happen if you disobey your boss's orders?"

"Definite suspension. Possible expulsion. Maybe even criminal charges."

"But would it end the world?" asked Lucifer.

"No, but there are other things to consider," said Isaiah.

"And this isn't just about me, it's also about my partner."

Lucifer stared intently into Isaiah's eyes. "Then let's make a deal."

Isaiah snickered. "Yeah, because that always works so well."

"I'm not talking some sort of demon deal. I couldn't care less about your damn soul," said Lucifer. "A gentleman's agreement."

Isaiah held out the cigarillo and watched as the smoke circled from the tip. "Okay, color me curious. Keep talking."

"You follow my lead. We go through the ritual, we summon Baron Samedi, and we find a way to stop Barbatos," said Lucifer.

"And in return…?" asked Isaiah.

"Once we've finished this, then you can do with me what you will."

Isaiah looked at the Morningstar. "You're serious? You'd surrender?"

"If that's what you want, then yes," said Lucifer. "I won't protest your decision in any way, shape, or form. If you want to take me into custody and present me to your superiors, if you want to blame me for pulling some sort of Jedi mind trick and hypnotizing you into this, then that's your choice. And I'll confess to whatever you want me to."

"What about the big guy? He doesn't seem like the surrender type."

"Belial's not involved in this."

"Bullshit," said Isaiah. "If we take you in, we can't have him running around out there. He's liable to come after you."

"No, he won't," said Lucifer. "You allow him to return to Hell and I promise he'll do nothing more. He'll also spread the word to any demons on Earth that I am to be left alone."

"What about all the demons still running around? The ones you set free when you came up here?" asked Isaiah.

"I'm confident your organization will have the resources to handle them yourselves. I'll even provide you with whatever assistance I can," said Lucifer. "I'd be the Hannibal Lecter to your Clarice Starling."

Isaiah raised an eyebrow. "You couldn't have gone with Will Graham?"

Lucifer scoffed. "It's a good deal, Agent. And I imagine being the man who captured the Devil would be a pretty impressive feather in your cap. What do you think?"

"Yeah, it'd certainly make me look good," said Isaiah. "What guarantees do I have that this isn't some trick?"

"I'm a man of my word, Agent Reeves." Lucifer extended his hand. "When you make an agreement with me, I will honor it."

"The Devil is telling me to trust him?" asked Isaiah. "You realize how that sounds, don't you?"

"All I have is my honor. You can either take a chance and go with me on this, or you can try to stop Barbatos on your own. But you can't do this without me and I certainly can't do it without you. Like it or not, the only option either of us has is to trust the other. So…?"

Isaiah looked down at Lucifer's open hand. If this didn't work, it would be catastrophic. Lucifer was right, though. There weren't any other options for him and Samara wouldn't sign off on the summoning unless he agreed to it, too. It was a risky gambit, probably the riskiest Isaiah would ever make. But he had to do it.

"Once the dust clears, you're mine."

Lucifer nodded.

"All right. I can't believe I'm doing this, but I'm in."

Isaiah took hold of Lucifer's hand and they shook.

CHAPTER 22

Samara had been busy looking over the books in the library when Lucifer and Isaiah returned. She pulled her attention from the leather spines and walked back to the couch.

"So are we all set?" she asked.

Belial, who had been standing at the window, turned around to focus his attention on the conversation.

Lucifer glanced at Isaiah. There was a moment's hesitation before he said, "Yeah, we're good."

Samara raised an eyebrow. "You sure about that?"

"Trust me, everything's fine," said Isaiah.

"Okay, so what's our plan?" she asked, resting her hands on her hips.

"You and I are going to call on the good Baron for a little meeting," said Lucifer. "We'll have a chat with him about what Barbatos's plan is. Hopefully get him to play along with us."

"You know if we do this, there's a pretty big risk," said Samara.

"I'm aware. But I have a feeling he'll want to hear what I have to say," said Lucifer.

"Still, there are some things we'll need to summon him.

I can make a list," said Samara. "Also, we're going to need rum and lots of it. Tobacco wouldn't hurt, either. Samedi's got a fondness for both."

"Make your list and Belial can procure whatever you need," said Lucifer. Belial gave a nod of understanding.

"While you're speaking with the Baron, what do you need from the rest of us?" asked Isaiah.

"There is something I'll need done, but it's very dangerous," said Lucifer.

"Well, don't keep me in suspense."

"If Barbatos were to get wind at all of what we're doing, he might try to stop us in some way," said Lucifer. "He needs to be distracted."

"You want to send Zay after the demon who nearly *killed* you?" asked Samara.

"I never said I wanted anything. In fact, I was planning to send Belial alone to keep Barbatos distracted," said Lucifer.

"I'll go with him," said Isaiah.

"He'll only slow me down," said Belial.

"I can't just sit here and do nothing," said Isaiah. "If I can help in some way, then that's what I've gotta do. Besides, I've been fighting demons for almost twenty years. I can hold my own."

"Not against this one," said Belial.

Isaiah grumbled. "Fine, then consider me a human shield."

Belial thought for a moment and then said, "That I can live with."

Samara moved from the couch and walked closer to Isaiah. When she spoke to him, her voice was a little lower. "You don't have to do this."

"I'm not gonna stand around feeling as useful as tits on a bull," said Isaiah. "I'll just go stir-crazy sitting on my hands, you know that."

Samara sighed, but she knew it was useless trying to talk Isaiah out of something once he had his mind made up. So instead, she gave a nod. "Fine, but if you get your ass killed, I'm going to be very pissed at you."

Isaiah chuckled. "Yeah, yeah. You gonna write up that list or what?"

Samara stuck out her tongue and then took out her phone. She typed up the list of things the spell required and texted it to her partner.

Isaiah took out his phone when he felt it vibrate. He opened up the text and read over the ingredients. "Okay, looks good. Should we get going?"

Lucifer nodded. "Yes, you take Belial, gather what we need. Then when you get back, we'll begin the spell while the two of you find Barbatos and keep him distracted."

"Will he still be in the same place?" asked Isaiah.

"Highly likely," said Belial. "And now that I've been there once, I can easily return. At the very least, it will give us a place to start. Come along."

Belial walked to the front door and Isaiah went after him. Once they heard the door close, Lucifer focused his attention on Samara. She had already returned to browsing the shelves.

"If there's anything you'd like to borrow, you're more than welcome," he said.

She glanced over her shoulder and gave a soft smile. "Thanks, but I don't got much time to read these days."

"Too busy saving the world?"

"Something like that." She turned her back on the

shelves. "Zay's not telling me something, is he?"

"What do you mean?"

"That hesitation when I asked him if everything was cool. What'd you two talk about?"

"I'm not going to divulge the contents of our conversation."

"OSIRIS didn't sanction this spell, did they? And he doesn't want me to know because in case they get wind of it, the hammer will just come down on him and not me."

"Is he wrong to try and protect you?"

"Kinda," she said. "I'm a big girl, I can take care of myself. But he likes to think of me as his little sister. Thinks it's his job to protect me. It's sweet, but it can also be condescending as all get out."

"Perhaps it's something the two of you should discuss," said Lucifer. "When things go unsaid, it can lead to issues later on down the line."

"I'll keep that in mind," said Samara. "So where are we going to do this? Right here?"

"No, I have a room downstairs. Follow me."

Lucifer beckoned her with a wave of his hand and led the way out of the library and into the foyer. He turned and walked down the hall beside the staircase. At the end of the hall was a door leading down to a darkened basement. Lucifer went first, turning on the lights as he descended the steps.

Once Samara reached the basement, she was surprised at what she saw. The basement almost seemed to resemble a dungeon. There was an altar against one of the walls. The other walls had shelves mounted to them and there were a number of different artifacts and ingredients used in a variety of spells. The floor was concrete and completely bare. No chairs of any kind, it seemed. She also noticed something on the wall space between the shelves.

"Wardings," said Lucifer. "From a mystical standpoint, this is the most secure room in the house. If something is summoned in here, it won't be getting out."

"But some of these wards I'm seeing…" she said. "Wouldn't these work on demons and angels?"

"Of course they would," said Lucifer.

"Then how do you—?"

"As I said before, I'm different," said Lucifer. "It's ironic when you think about it. When the Divine Choir cast me out of Heaven, they wanted me to keep my wings as a reminder of what I'd lost. I was no longer an angel, but I also wasn't quite a demon, either. But what I doubt they knew at the time was that they were also stripping me of the weaknesses of both races."

"Guess they didn't think that one through, did they?" said Samara.

"Suppose not," said Lucifer. "So, what do you think? Are these accommodations suitable?"

Samara continued looking around the room. "Yeah, I think so. I'll go get my things and then once Belial and Zay get back, we can start working on the preparations."

She started to climb the steps, but Lucifer called to her before she got very far.

"Agent Tillman?" he asked. "You said this is uncharted territory for you. Are you sure you're up for it? I might have some other contacts I can reach out to if you're not."

Samara turned, leaning on the stair's handrail. "If I'm being honest, I really don't know. But we also don't know how far ahead of us Barbatos is. What if we don't have time to find someone else?"

"If I had the option…I mean, if I still had my powers…"

She nodded. "I know. It's a fight you'd be happy to wage solo. But we gotta play the hand we're dealt, don't we?"

"I suppose so," he said. "Go on, get your things. Like you said, we don't know how much time we've actually got."

CHAPTER 23

The summoning circle was complete, with lit candles placed around it. A box of cigars and a bottle of Barbancourt were inside the circle, as was a chalice. Lucifer ignored the clucking sound that came from the tiny cage just outside the circle. He heard footsteps and looked to the staircase to see Samara descending the steps. She wore a white toga and her hair was covered up by a white bandana.

"Is this part of the ritual?" asked Lucifer.

"No, I just don't want to get any blood in my hair or on my clothes," said Samara as she moved barefoot over to the circle. She took a sheathed knife from the folds of her clothing and drew the blade, the knelt down and set the weapon in front of her.

Belial and Isaiah were able to acquire everything on Samara's list. There weren't that many ingredients, but they were key.

"This will work?" asked Lucifer.

"It's all in the offering," she said. "You have to give him something he'd be interested in."

Samara reached for the cage and opened it, slowly reaching inside to pull out the rooster. The bird, perhaps sensing the intent, started to flap his wings and wiggle. Samara spoke to him in a soothing voice and gently rubbed his back. This seemed to calm the bird, at least for now.

"Doesn't seem like a very sanitary fellow if this is how he prefers his meat," said Lucifer.

"I don't make the rules. Once he turns up, you two can swap recipes."

"Is there anything else I should know?" asked Lucifer.

"He's something of a character. Even if you find him offensive, don't let him get to you," said Samara. "But don't lie to him, either. He'll know and then God help you."

Lucifer bristled at the warning but said nothing else.

As Samara continued to speak in a soothing tone to the rooster, she kept one hand firmly on the back of his neck. She rubbed it, and the rubbing became progressively harder. Then she grabbed the neck tightly.

The rooster now began fearing for his life and started to struggle. But the effort was wasted. Samara was calm and deliberate in her motions, reaching out with her free hand for the knife. Carefully, Samara took the knife in hand and then drew it quickly across the rooster's throat. She held the bird over the chalice, allowing his blood to flow freely from the cut, spilling over her fingers, and landing into the bowl.

She laid what remained of the rooster in the circle and then picked up the chalice with both hands and passed it to Lucifer. He took it and set it on the ground. Then, Samara passed him the knife. Lucifer accepted it and carefully cut across his palm. He held the closed fist over the chalice and squeezed, allowing his own blood to drip into the cup and mix with the animal's.

Samara picked up the chalice once again and bowed her head as she raised it up. "These offerings are for the patriarch of the Guédé Family. Baron Samedi, one of the sky children requests an audience with you. Should you honor our request, we promise these humble offerings as recompense."

The candles flickered as a cool chill swept through the room. Samara kept her eyes closed and began to sing in a low voice. As the lyrics flowed from her lips, so too the wind grew stronger. Soon, Lucifer could feel the presence of another in the basement. He rose from his knees and looked around, but the wind prevented the candles from truly illuminating anything.

The flames blew out and the scent of their burnt wicks hung in the air.

And then, a new flame was birthed, not far from where the circle was. This flame came from a pair of tall torches that stood on either side of the shadowy figure. He leaned against the wall, his arms folded in front of his chest, and the brim of a top hat hiding his eyes.

"So, seems someone wanted an audience," he said in a voice that was smooth but also with a hint of malice. He tipped the hat back as he looked up. A white skull was painted over his face and he wore a pair of sunglasses, but the lens on the left eye was missing. Through that missing lens, Lucifer could see an eye with an emerald glow to it. He wore a black tuxedo and stepped out from the torches. His right hand rested atop a walking stick, which had the head of a crystal skull.

Once he moved to the circle, he stopped and looked down. He pointed the stick at the bottle of rum and the box of cigars, then moved his green eye between the pair? "For *moi*?"

"A gift," said Samara, standing from the circle. "For coming all this way, Baron."

Samedi rested his cane against the wall, then stepped into the circle and crouched, picking up the bottle first. He unscrewed the top and took a sniff of the contents. Samedi wrapped his lips around the opening and tipped the bottle back, chugging a decent amount of the rum. He took the bottle from his mouth and gave a satisfied smack of his lips.

"Not bad," he said. "I've had better, but I've also had a lot goddamn fuckin' worse."

He opened the cigar box and took one of them out, placing it under his nose and giving it several good, long sniffs. Samedi bit the end off the cigar and spat it against the far wall, then placed it between his lips. He produced a wooden match out of what seemed like thin air, struck it against the concrete floor, and held the flame over the cigar's edge. Once the tobacco leaves caught the flame, he shook the match and stood. The cigar held in one hand, the bottle of rum in the other.

"Thanks for the gifts," he said as he started to walk back to the two torches.

"Where are you going?" asked Lucifer.

Samedi stopped and glanced over his shoulder. "Home. Why, you wanna snuggle first?"

"Does this look like the corner liquor store?" asked Lucifer. "We didn't summon you just for some booze and cigars. We summoned you for a real reason."

"'Summon'?" asked Samedi, sliding his sunglasses down the bridge of his nose. The green eye flashed with anger, but his other eye remained in deep shadow. Lucifer briefly wondered if there even *was* a second eye. "No one *summons* the Baron, my brother. I am *called upon* and then

I choose for myself whether or not I will show. Sometimes, I don't. Other times, I do—but just to claim my offering."

"Maybe I can offer you much more than just a bottle of rum and a box of cigars."

"Really?" Samedi faced Lucifer. "And just what would that be?"

The corner of Lucifer's mouth curled into a slight smirk. "Your freedom."

Baron Samedi simply paused, staring at Lucifer in silence. A lifetime seemed to pass in those moments. Two supernatural titans standing off against each other as if it were a western. And then, finally, one of them cracked.

Laughter erupted from Baron Samedi's mouth, echoing through the dungeon-esque basement. He cackled for so long and with such intensity, Lucifer wondered when the loa would ever just shut up.

"Are you done?" the Morningstar finally asked with exasperation.

Samedi stopped laughing, but the smile remained and his body shook with suppressed amusement. "You make me laugh, brother. So for that shit, I'll stay a spell. What do you fuckin' want?"

"I don't suppose you know who I am."

Samedi looked him up and down, then shrugged. "All you white boys look the same to me. You someone famous or somethin'?"

"You might say that," said Lucifer. "I'm the Morning-star."

Silence again filled the air, punctuated almost immediately by more laughter from the Baron.

"How fucking stupid do you think I am?" asked Baron

Samedi. "The Morningstar, he don't leave his tropical retirement home. Nobody seen him set foot outside of Hell in centuries."

"It's true, Baron," said Samara, then nodded in Lucifer's direction. "This *is* the Morningstar."

"Is he, now?" Samedi took a few long puffs on the cigar and then moved closer to Lucifer. He stared at him carefully with the glowing eye and then took a few good sniffs of him. "Then how come I don't smell no sulfur on him?"

"Because we're in a rather unique situation here," said Lucifer. "I've lost my abilities. For all intents and purposes, I am human."

"If your ass is human and sittin' up here on Earth, then that means some other bastard's runnin' Hell, don' it?"

Lucifer nodded.

"All right, then you got nothin' of interest for me." Samedi tipped his hat. "Thanks again for the presents."

"Why would you leave without hearing me out?" asked Lucifer.

Samedi sighed and turned around. He plucked the cigar from his mouth and leaned against the wall. After a drink of rum, he puffed on the cigar some more, savoring the mixture of rum and tobacco before he spoke again.

"Humans, they provide entertainment. They understand the concept of deals. Celestials, they only useful when they have something to trade. A powerless celestial is about as useful as a eunuch in a whore house."

"Eunuchs were frequently used as guards in such places, so seems they did have a purpose," chided Lucifer.

Samedi smirked at the response. "Okay, you know how to talk. So for that, I give you one minute. Thrill me, Mr. S."

"There's a demon who has escaped from Hell, one who wishes to use necromancy to resurrect all the corpses on Earth. Have them destroy humanity."

Samedi gave a shrug. "So what you worried about? Thing like that ain't possible. Only a small number of people in all creation who've got the power to do something like that."

"And you're one of them," said Lucifer.

Samedi bowed his head in acknowledgment. "Guilty."

"Which means that you're a target," said Lucifer. "This demon, Barbatos, plans to somehow get his hands on your power. And he was confident he could do it."

Samedi gave a scoff. "Like I said, you got nothin' to worry your little hooves. There ain't a thing that can contain me."

"You're lying," said Lucifer.

Samedi cocked a brow. "You callin' me a liar, boy?"

"I know how the universe works, Baron," said Lucifer, locking eyes with the loa and not backing down an inch. "How it *really* works. There is no such thing as omnipotence. For every force, there is a counter. You are but a servant of Death. One of his many avatars that walks the Earth in his place. And you too are capable of being contained and controlled."

Samedi held the cigar right in front of his lips, just staring at Lucifer in what could almost be classified as a state of paralysis. Then finally, he just gave a defiant shake of his head.

"No...not possible...he couldn't..."

"I know my demons, Baron," said Lucifer. "Barbatos would not be so confident unless he had a reason to be. He's found something, some way to control your power.

If I had my own abilities, I'd do something to stop it. But as you pointed out, I'm not much use for the time being."

Samedi sighed and walked over to the altar in the corner of the room. He hopped up on it and perched himself on its surface. After taking another long drink of his rum, he gave a sigh.

"So seems we got ourselves a situation then, don't it? And what do you expect me to do about this? If he's already got a means of controllin' me…"

"His plan hinges on his ability to summon and contain you," said Lucifer. "But if we removed you from the equation, he can't complete his plan."

Samedi laughed. "Yeah, that's a good one. 'Cept how you gonna take ol' Baron Samedi from the board? I can't be killed, fam."

"Maybe not, but your power can be transferred," said Lucifer.

"Wait, what?" asked Samara, grabbing Lucifer's shoulder. "You never said anything about that!"

"I said I'd try to make a deal with the Baron. I never specified *what* the deal would be."

"Seems there's some dissent in your ranks," said Samedi.

"Damn right there is!" said Samara. "What the hell kind of game are you playing, Lucifer? You can't honestly expect me to stand by and do nothing as you take the power of a loa for your own!"

"I'm not interested in permanently claiming his power," said Lucifer. "I just want to borrow it. Just long enough so we can stop Barbatos. After that, the good Baron will have his power restored."

"And what do I get in return?" asked Samedi.

"For one, Death doesn't scatter your atoms across the

universe for your failure to stop a demon from destroying humanity."

"Not a bad opener," said Samedi. "But the pot, you gonna have to sweeten it. Y'see, I like takin' chances in my life."

"I'm aware of that."

Lucifer moved closer to Samedi and bent down in front of him. He whispered something that Samara was incapable of hearing. And as the words passed from Lucifer's lips, the smile on the Baron's face began to grow.

"Oh, that's a good one. That sounds like a good spot of fun to be had..."

Once Lucifer finished, Samedi rose to his feet.

"What do you say?" asked Lucifer.

"I say let's get started." Samedi held out his fist and Lucifer bumped it with his own.

CHAPTER 24

In the short period Isaiah had known Belial, he'd experienced the effects of teleportation a few times. When Belial transported them from Metairie to Lucifer's home in Chicago, when they went out to search for the supplies Samara needed, and now again returning to this big cat sanctuary where Barbatos was last located.

And each time, Isaiah felt like his stomach was going to leap into his throat.

It wasn't a pleasant experience and the OSIRIS agent wondered if it were possible to ever get used to the effect. He bent over, one hand rubbing his stomach, just waiting to see if anything would come up.

"You mortals have such weak organs," said Belial.

"No argument from me on that point." Isaiah dry-heeved a few times and then righted himself. "Okay, think I'm good."

He looked at the front entrance of the sanctuary. There was a wooden sign boarded up over the front entrance that read "CLOSED UNTIL FURTHER NOTICE." Isaiah walked up to the sign and tugged on it a few times, but it wouldn't come loose.

"Seems Barbatos doesn't want any visitors."

Belial moved behind Isaiah. "Step aside."

The agent did as he was told and the demon came up to the entrance. He drove his fist through the sign and the front door, then pulled the door from its hinges and casually walked inside. Isaiah reached under his jacket and drew his gun, following Belial.

Through the small lobby and past the offices, they came to the park entrance. Paths leading visitors through the caged areas where the cats roamed. Or at least in theory. But they saw no sign of any creature in the enclosures.

"Is he even here?" asked Isaiah.

"Yes," said Belial. "I can sense his presence."

"Okay, so where's he—"

Isaiah didn't have a chance to finish that sentence. Right in front of him, Belial's shape twisted. The skin melted from his face, dripping off bit by bit and falling into puddles on the ground. Horns emerged from his forehead, curving as they grew in length. His ears spiked and when he spoke, a forked tongue flickered between his lips, which curled to reveal ivory fangs. That provided a sharp contrast to the dark-red skin.

"What the hell is going on?" asked Isaiah, stepping away from the demon and bringing up his weapon.

"What do you think?"

Isaiah spun on his heel and swung his weapon around. Perched atop one of the fences was a man with long, dark hair and a goatee, wearing a simple pair of dark slacks and nothing else. He flipped from one fence to the other across the way, moving too fast for Isaiah to really keep a bead on.

Then he jumped again, but this time he paused at the apex and feathered wings emerged from his back. They gently brought him lower until his bare feet touched the ground. When he looked at Isaiah, it was with bright, blue eyes.

"This isn't happening…" muttered Isaiah, keeping the gun trained on him.

"Oh yes it is, Agent Reeves."

He reached a hand out and placed it on Isaiah's gun. Gently but still with sufficient strength, he pushed down on the gun and Isaiah found his arm dropping to his side.

"I am Barbatos and I am an angel sent by Heaven."

"You're lying."

"Am I?" Barbatos held his arms out to the sides in a gesture that guided Isaiah's eyes to look at the wingspan. "Think about what makes more sense to you, Agent Reeves. That the Devil and his demon henchman would come to Earth to capture other demons—all of whom are devoted to his cause, might I add. Or that he's been playing you this whole time, casting spells and manipulating you."

"Nice try, but I'm not falling for it," said Isaiah. "I was in Metairie. I've seen your handiwork."

"You mean you've seen *Lucifer's* handiwork," said Barbatos. "Please don't tell me you actually *believed* his sob story?"

"I…I don't…" Isaiah stammered as Barbatos continued to speak.

"The greatest trick the Devil ever pulled used to be convincing the world that he didn't exist. But now, he's managed to convince people that *he's* actually the hero in this little drama. And it's given him the power to operate with impunity, to corrupt more human souls to his cause."

"But…"

The more Barbatos explained, the harder Isaiah was finding it to deny his words. Of course, it all made sense now. Isaiah himself had spent his entire career with OSIRIS hunting down and killing demons. If Lucifer gave a damn about rogue demons running loose, how come he never did anything to stop all those others?

But what if he was just using that as a pretext? Maybe Barbatos wasn't a demon at all. Maybe he was actually an angel, just as he said. And it all started to make more sense.

"Look at that weapon of yours, Agent Reeves," said Barbatos. "What does it do?"

Isaiah raised the gun, examining the runes engraved on the barrel. His gaze drifted from the weapon and met Barbatos's beautiful, cobalt eyes.

"It kills demons."

Barbatos nodded. "And what is your job?"

"I…I work for OSIRIS. We investigate the supernatural."

"And? When you find a demon, what do you do? Do you join forces with it?"

"No," said Isaiah, and then after a beat and with more conviction, "*Hell* no!"

Barbatos nodded his head in a gesture. "There. Behind you."

Isaiah turned around and looked back at Belial, still in demonic form and seemingly frozen in time. "What's happened to him?"

"We're between moments in time right now," said Barbatos. "The power of Heaven has shown you Belial's true form. You see him for what he is, don't you?"

Isaiah nodded his head. "You're right, I see him."

"What is he?"

"A demon."

"And what do you do to demons, Agent Reeves?"

Isaiah turned in Belial's direction and he slowly brougt his gun up, holding it at arm's length and pointing the barrel right at Belial's head. His finger rubbed the trigger as his eyes narrowed in determination.

"I blow the motherfuckers away."

"So go, then. Do what you were meant to do."

Isaiah smiled as he squeezed the trigger. Everything seemed to move in slow-motion—the explosion from the barrel that caused the runes all along the gun to flash just briefly, the bullet escaping the confines of the gun, and then Isaiah watched, waiting for the bullet to find its mark in the head of the demon.

But it didn't. Something grabbed hold of Isaiah's wrist. That invisible force twisted Isaiah's arm behind his back, applying pressure until he couldn't maintain his grip on the weapon. It fell and hit the paved walkway, while Isaiah was raised off the ground and pinned against the fence.

The world returned to normal and he saw not the face of a demon, but Belial's human form once more. He had one hand on Isaiah's wrist, the other around his throat. But his yellow eyes didn't seem angry, just confused.

"Why did you attack me?" asked Belial. "I thought we had a deal?"

"I…" Isaiah struggled to remember what had just transpired between them, but his memory was suddenly covered in a dense fog. "I have no idea what you're talking about? Last thing I remember was feeling sick after you teleported me here."

Belial leaned closer and gave a few sniffs.

"Are you—" Isaiah's face contorted into an expression of disgust and bewilderment "—*smelling* me?"

"Barbatos," hissed Belial. "I can smell his stench on you."

"The hell does *that* mean?"

"It means he possessed you, if only for a moment," said Belial. "He knows we're here and he's going to try to use you against me."

"Okay, so what now?"

Belial set Isaiah back on solid ground and said, "Now you leave."

Isaiah shook his head. "That's not an option."

Belial turned away from the agent and continued down the path. "I can't locate Barbatos while also keeping an eye on you. I appreciate your help up until this point, Agent Reeves, but you just became a liability."

Isaiah picked up his gun and pointed it at Belial's back. The demon sighed and turned around. "You couldn't manage to kill me even while you were possessed. What makes you think you can do it when you're in full control of your own body?"

"We got a job to finish and I aim to do just that," said Isaiah. "Now either we work together on this or you can just kill my ass right here, right now."

"Fine."

In the blink of an eye, Belial was right in front of Isaiah. Once more, one hand took hold of the agent's wrist, keeping the gun pointed towards the sky. But the other hand, that he placed on Isaiah's chest. The sound of sizzling meat combined with the stench of human flesh filled the air. The spot where Belial's hand rested was the source of searing pain that nearly drove Isaiah to his knees. It felt like someone had placed a hot iron right on his chest.

Belial pulled the hand away and Isaiah almost collapsed,

needing to use the fence to steady himself. He looked at the spot where Belial's hand had been, but there wasn't a mark on his clothes. Isaiah unbuttoned his shirt and pulled it open so he could get a look at his chest. There, right above his heart, was a sigil burned into his flesh. It still held a slight glow and smoke wafted up from the fresh mark.

"The...the fuck did you do to me?" asked Isaiah.

"You said the choices were to either kill you or work with you. The only way I could work with you was if I knew you wouldn't be a threat," said Belial, turning back to the path. "That brand binds us together. Now, no demon in creation can possess you."

"Hang on, 'binds'?" asked Isaiah, buttoning his shirt back up and following Belial. "The hell does that mean?"

"Relax. All it means is that we are connected."

"Well take it off!"

"I can't, the mark is permanent," said Belial. "Think of it as a...friendship brand."

Isaiah's face burned with anger. "Friends don't *brand* each other."

"You should be thanking me, Agent Reeves. Now, demons will have reason to fear you because you are the only human who bears the mark of Hell's bounty hunter," said Belial.

It seemed useless to pursue the matter further. While not being at risk of possession was a definite benefit, Isaiah was afraid of what this connection might mean going forward.

Belial led the way down the path through the caged areas and Isaiah could only follow. He hated every inch of this place, hated that he was putting his career at risk like this, hated that he'd put Samara in a position to perform a dangerous spell, and now hated that he was apparently blood brothers with one of the most dangerous demons in Hell.

Their trek eventually brought them to a locked door that read "STAFF ONLY." Belial ignored it and burst in. Isaiah followed behind, his gun held at the ready. And inside, they saw they were in a large enclosure, possibly where the animals were fed. There was a group of tigers off to one side. They stared at the two intruders with murderous intent, some even licking their lips in anticipation. But they didn't strike, just remained still lying on the concrete.

In the center of the large habitat was a chair. Crudely constructed and Barbatos sat upon it. His wings were extended, though now Isaiah could see them as the leathery versions they really were, not the angelic feathered ones he saw before.

"Such a shame that you wouldn't do as you were told, Agent Reeves," said Barbatos. "Now I see you've become Belial's little puppet."

"Surrender now, Barbatos," said Belial. "And I swear to you on the name of the Morningstar that I shall make your execution a quick one."

"Oh, of course. I'd be happy to surrender to you, brother," said Barbatos. "But you will have to wait until *after* I've completed my plan."

Barbatos made a gesture to the side. There were a few tigers who sat there and they parted with a wave of Barbatos's hand, revealing a summoning circle.

"Once I've finished my work and raised every human corpse from its grave, then you can kill me," said Barbatos. "By that point, my work will have been done and I'll have nothing else to live for."

CHAPTER 25

saiah squeezed off a few shots just as one of the tigers rushed him. But the beast was too swift and each of his bullets missed the mark. The tiger leapt, claws bared and jaw open. Isaiah brought up an arm to defend himself and closed his eyes.

Then he heard a yelp. When Isaiah lowered his arms, he saw the tiger had been lassoed by a flaming rope. Belial gripped the other end of the rope, yanking back on it to pull the tiger away. He pulled hard and there was a loud crack before the cat's body went limp.

The rest of the group went for Belial instead, rightly seeing him as the more immediate threat. Now Isaiah had a better chance and without the fear of an imminent mauling to throw off his aim. He aimed carefully and squeezed off a few shots, taking down one of the tigers.

Three were left and the gunshot drew their attention. Isaiah's distraction gave Belial a chance to pounce himself. At the apex of his jump, he held his hands above his head and hellfire swirled around them. Amazement filled Isaiah's eyes as he watched the otherworldly flames flow from within the demon's body and forging into the shape of a broadsword.

Belial fell upon one of the tigers, the hellfire sword skewering it through the back. The tiger let out one final yelp before it collapsed. Belial hurled the sword through the air and it split into two smaller daggers that impaled the remaining animals.

Isaiah was stunned by what he'd just seen. He'd fought demons before, but none of them had been capable of using hellfire. Watching the way Belial could wield such power with that level of skill was unreal to the OSIRIS agent.

But he had to be torn from his momentary trance almost as quickly as he fell into it. Belial shouted something and Isaiah realized the demon was looking *past* him. The agent spun around and saw just what he meant.

The tigers were just there to distract them so Barbatos could begin his own ritual. He stood inside the summoning circle, holding up a chalice filled with what seemed to be blood, and drank it down. Barbatos shouted something in an ancient, unfamiliar language and the lit candles that lined the circle exploded into towering jet-streams of fire.

Barbatos's laughter echoed through the enclosure as the air in front of him became distorted. A tear opened in the fabric of time and space, expanding larger until a figure stepped forth, wearing a tuxedo and a top hat. The new arrival had his head dipped low, one hand resting on a cane topped with a crystal skull.

Barbatos stepped out of the circle, blood still dribbling down his chin, and knelt before the black-clad figure. "Baron Samedi, it is an honor to be graced by your presence. And together, I believe I have a proposition for you that will—"

"You can spare your propositions, Barbatos." The figure removed the hat and looked up, revealing the face of Lucifer, with a skull painted over it. "No one here is interested in what you have to say."

"Lucifer…?" Barbatos's face was stricken with not only confusion but also a touch of fear. "This isn't possible, I summoned—"

"You thought you would summon Baron Samedi, and chain him to you with a spell you somehow discovered in Cocytus." Lucifer calmly crossed the distance to the summoning circle. "Unfortunately for you, that spell would only work on the Baron himself. So I invited him to my place for a little chat. And we came to an agreement, where he'd bestow his powers upon me for a period of twenty-four hours."

"In exchange for what?" asked Barbatos. "Samedi wouldn't just sign over his power to you without getting something in return. What did you promise him?"

"Sorry, but I can't tell you that," said Lucifer. "Devil-client privilege, you know."

"Fine, no matter." Barbatos clasped his hands together while his eyes flared up with yellow light, burning hotly in the enclosure. He pulled his hands apart, a hellfire sword forming between his palms. Barbatos took hold of the blade and readied himself for combat. "Maybe you have Samedi's powers, but you're not skilled in them. Not enough to stop me from cutting your fucking head off!"

Lucifer tossed the hat to the side, stripped off his jacket, and unbuttoned then rolled his sleeves. He held out one hand and motioned for Barbatos to come at him.

The demon accepted the invite with exuberance. His wings propelled him at Lucifer, but the Morningstar deflected the first attempted strike with Samedi's cane. A few more swipes were stopped with that cane, and then Lucifer twirled it. He swung the weapon and the crystal skull made contact with Barbatos's head.

Lucifer circled behind while Barbatos was stunned and got in a few more hits. Barbatos's anger was clearly flaring up and he turned and grabbed both of Lucifer's wrists. With anger burning in his eyes, Barbatos's wings carried the two of them above and his hands pumped hellfire into Lucifer's body.

There had been many times when Lucifer had used hellfire on others. When it was used on him, it could be painful, depending on the strength of the demon. But without any vestiges of his former power, now he was completely at the mercy.

And the hellfire *burned*. It poured over his soul like a tidal wave, hitting him with pulse after pulse of searing intensity. The Morningstar had never realized just how devastating hellfire could be to a soul until that moment. With each cascade that was thrown directly at him, Lucifer's doubts and insecurities clawed their way to the fore of his brain. He was reminded of each failure he'd endured over his long life.

Lucifer screamed, but Barbatos wouldn't let go. On the ground, Isaiah Reeves felt like a helpless bystander. But he looked down at his gun. It was a long shot, yet he felt he had to do something. Isaiah took aim, lining up his sights with the demon. At this range and with so much on the line, he wanted to be sure he would hit Barbatos and not Lucifer. But the flailing made it hard to get a fix. Isaiah took a deep breath and squeezed the trigger.

The bullet struck its mark and though it didn't kill Barbatos, it did give him a moment's distraction and the hellfire ceased. Belial jumped into the air, his own wings expanding and he grabbed Barbatos, tearing him away from Lucifer. The two demons crashed right through the enclosure's ceiling.

Without any wings of his own, the Morningstar fell right back down. Isaiah went over to him, but by the time he reached, Lucifer was already rising back to his feet and dusting off his clothing.

"That was embarrassing…" He then acknowledged Isaiah. "Thank you."

"What now?" asked Isaiah.

"Now, I have to finish this." Lucifer picked up his cane and held it out in front of him. He drew it across the empty air, and a tear in reality opened in its wake. "Come along, just a quick jump."

Lucifer waved in the direction of the portal. Isaiah gave him a concerned look, but the determination in the Morningstar's skull-painted face suggested he believed it to be safe. So Isaiah walked through and Lucifer followed.

In the blink of an eye, they were outside again. Belial and Barbatos were flying high above, exchanging bursts of hellfire and rushing at each other wth flaming swords and daggers. But neither one seemed to really get the upper hand.

"Belial!" shouted Lucifer, from the ground. "Stop messing around and bring him down here!"

Belial followed the instructions, barreling into Barbatos and flying him towards the ground. They crashed just a few feet away from Lucifer, lying in the center of a freshly born crater.

Belial had Barbatos by the throat and Lucifer calmly stepped up to him. He patted Belial on the shoulder and the demon apparently took that as an order to stand aside.

Belial released Barbatos and let him slip to the ground.

"You think you've won, Lucifer? This is just a setback," said Barbatos. "You don't have the power to send me back to Cocytus."

"You're right, I don't," said Lucifer. "Which is why we aren't going to Cocytus."

"Wait…what?"

Both of Lucifer's hands tightened around the cane. He raised it into the air and drove the tip right into Barbatos's chest. The demon screamed and the world melted away for them both, and they soon found themselves in a new realm. A large expanse of green with trees dotting the landscape and cliffs and mountains off in the places where the sun didn't touch.

Lucifer stepped back and removed the cane. Barbatos looked down at his chest and saw no wound. He got to his feet and looked around the new environment.

"Where are we?" he asked.

"A place called Ginen," said Lucifer. "I think you'll like it here. Particularly when you meet who you'll be staying with."

A cacophony of caws spooked Barbatos and as he strained to find the source, he saw that the shadows where the mountains and cliffs rested were actually comprised of thousands—perhaps millions—of ravens. The carrion birds swarmed Barbatos, zipping by him in flashing blurs. Wave after wave, and each one seemed to tear at his demonic wings, until they were nothing but bones with flecks of skin still clinging.

"You can't do this to me, Lucifer!" cried Barbatos.

"Me?" asked Lucifer. "I'm not doing a thing to you. I'm just the escort who brought you here."

The birds swarmed again and this time, their cawing sounded remarkably like a twisted cackle. Barbatos screamed, but his cry was drowned out by the laughter.

The birds flew up into the sky and left behind no trace of Barbatos. They circled around and came right back, hitting the grasslands where Lucifer stood. When they touched ground, they all seemed to merge together into one mass that took the shape of Baron Samedi.

"I see the legends are true, you are a man of your word," said Samedi. "It's been a pleasure doing business with you, Morningstar."

"And you, Baron," said Lucifer with a graceful nod. "I appreciate your assistance in this matter."

"Oh no, that was not assistance." Samedi held up a finger. "Remember, we have a deal. And one day, I will collect on this deal. Do we understand each other, Morningstar?"

"I wouldn't have it any other way," said Lucifer. "Now if you'll excuse me, I'd like to get back and tie up some loose ends before your powers return home."

Samedi gave a nod and a bow. "By all means. Enjoy them while you can, my friend. We will be in touch."

EPILOGUE

With Barbatos gone, no further corpses were raised in Metairie or New Orleans. Lucifer and the two OSIRIS agents remained in town just to be certain of that much. And once the Baron's powers had faded, Lucifer was convinced the ordeal was at last finished.

But before they parted ways, Isaiah had offered to treat Lucifer to dinner as a way of saying thank you. And that was what brought the three of them back to the same restaurant where they had first met, with Lucifer finally having the opportunity to finish the jambalaya this time.

"I'm still trying to figure out just what exactly we're going to tell our bosses," said Isaiah. "Not like we can just say that we helped the Devil and a loa capture a rogue demon. Right, Samara?"

"Definitely not."

That was a sampling of how talkative Samara Tillman had been all throughout dinner. Isaiah had done most of the talking for all three of them. But while Lucifer's silence was out of genuine interest in Isaiah's stories, he sensed it wasn't the same for Samara. More than few times, he could feel her hard glare on him.

"Spare some of the details, then," said Lucifer. "You

tell him you worked with a freelance warlock who was also in town investigating the case. Together, you were able to banish the demon."

"Thought you didn't lie," said Isaiah.

"Where's the lie in that explanation?" asked Lucifer.

Isaiah rolled the explanation a few times in his head while he chewed down a spoonful of his own jambalaya. After thinking it over, he gave a hesitant nod. "Suppose it could work…" He glanced at his partner. "What do you think?"

Samara shrugged. "Sounds fine."

Lucifer's eyes drifted to his watch. "Look at the time. I believe my ride will be here soon to take me back to Chicago."

Isaiah wiped his lips with his napkin while glancing at his own wrist. "Yeah, we should probably hit the road ourselves. Knowing HQ, they've probably already got another case lined up for us. So what do you say, partner? Ready to hit the road?"

"Sure, it's a long flight back to DC," said Samara.

The three of them rose from the table and after paying the bill at the register, gathered outside the front door of the restaurant. Belial was already standing and waiting, keeping a watchful eye on everyone who walked in front of the restaurant.

"It was…interesting to say the least." Isaiah shook Lucifer's hand. "I'm not saying we should do it again anytime soon…but it wouldn't be the worst thing in the world if our paths crossed."

"Agreed," said Lucifer as he returned the handshake.

"And I've got a…bond of some sort with the big guy anyway," said Isaiah as he gave Belial a simple pat on the arm. "Not sure how I'm gonna explain *that* one next time I'm at the gym, but figure I'll think of something."

Belial grunted a farewell to Isaiah as he started walking to the car.

Samara came up to Lucifer next and shook his hand. As she did, she leaned in close and whispered to him. "I'm not cool with the way you used me back there. So no matter what Zay says, my advice would be to keep your distance from us."

"Understood," said Lucifer.

She said nothing more to him or Belial and turned to join Isaiah at their car. Lucifer stepped beside Belial and the two watched as the OSIRIS agents drove off into the night.

"I heard what she said to you," said Belial. "Think she might be a problem down the line?"

"I doubt it. Seemed like human posturing more than anything else," said Lucifer. "How did you like it? Working so closely with regular humans?"

"They're soft and easy to kill," said Belial. "But there's a certain courage they possess. Despite the odds against him and how futile his actions were, Reeves still made an attempt to help us both."

"I suppose that's the closest you get to thanking a human, so it's something," said Lucifer. "Besides, we've more important things to concentrate on."

"Such as…?"

"Samedi's power is gone, he won't lend it to me again. And I can't go after any other of the escapees as a mortal," said Lucifer. "No, I need to get my powers back. And it seems increasingly likely that they won't simply return on their own. I'll have to take action."

"What do you mean?" asked Belial.

"I mean I have to go on a little journey," said Lucifer. "To the last place I ever wanted to return to again."

Belial faced his master, the look on his face almost approaching joy. "Are you saying what I think you're saying?"

"I am." Lucifer took a deep breath and sighed. "Whatever's happened to my powers, I think the only way I can even begin searching for answers to restore them is where they came from. That means I have to return to Hell."

AFTERWORD

Writing sequels can be hard. You don't want to just do the same thing as the first book all over again, because that's boring not only for the writer, but for the readers, too. So whenever I sit down to start planning a sequel, I always wonder what can I do this time that will be different from the previous book.

For Lucifer, I thought about what he was like in *Lucifer Rising*. He was arrogant, prideful, but he'd come to accept a sense of responsibility for his actions. And as Stan Lee and Steve Ditko taught us many decades ago, "with great power comes great responsibility."

But what happens when that power is gone? It's one thing to want to make amends when you have the power to do it. Does that same drive still exist once that power is stripped? The idea of Lucifer running around out there without the benefit of his powers opened up some new possibilities, and forced him to rely on other people.

It was a fun approach to take with this book. And it proved different from my initial idea (which I'm not going to tell you, because it might turn up again in the future). Now it also opens two other possibilities.

One is OSIRIS. I've been thinking about having some

sort of supernatural task force in the Dark Crossroads universe ever since the *Luther Cross* books. And you'll probably see them pop up again in the future.

The other is the third book, which at the time of this writing is tentatively titled *Lucifer Damned*. After he's turned the throne over to someone else, is it possible for Lucifer to go back to Hell and just get what he wants without problem?

Well, there wouldn't be much of a story in that, would there?

Thanks as always for reading, and I'll see you in the next book.

Percival Constantine
October 2020
Kagoshima, Japan

ABOUT THE AUTHOR

Born and raised in the Chicagoland area, Percival Constantine grew up on a fairly consistent diet of superhero comics, action movies, video games, and TV shows. At the age of ten, he first began writing and has never really stopped.

Percival has been working in publishing since 2005 in various capacities—author, editor, formatter, letterer—and has written books, short stories, comics, and more. He has a Bachelor of Arts in English and Mass Media from Northeastern Illinois University and a Master of Arts in English and Screenwriting from Southern New Hampshire University. He currently resides in southern Japan, where he teaches literature and film while continuing to write.

CONTINUE THE ADVENTURE!

MORNINGSTAR
BOOK 3

LUCIFER
DAMNED

PERCIVAL CONSTANTINE

NOW AVAILABLE IN PRINT AND DIGITAL

Printed in Great Britain
by Amazon

75422730R00132